Dangerous Stakes
A Detective Liv DeMarco Thriller

G.K. Parks

Copyright © 2019 G.K. Parks

A Modus Operandi imprint

All rights reserved.

ISBN: 1-942710-16-X
ISBN-13: 978-1-942710-16-5

For my mom and dad

OTHER BOOKS BY G.K. PARKS:

ONE

A streak of yellow caught his eye. His pulse quickened. It was almost time. He knew he had to be patient. He couldn't risk getting caught, not after all the planning and preparation that went into this.

The yellow sports car whipped around the curb and slid to a stop in front of the valet stand. The parking attendant came around, opening the driver's door. He watched the owner step out of the car and go inside the hotel. This would be easy.

For a moment, he felt overheated, a combination of fear and excitement. The tingles raced up and down his spine. He was ready. He gripped the steering wheel harder to control the twitching, his knuckles turning white. The sudden adrenaline surge made his mind focus. He stared at the car, willing it to move.

And when it did, he pulled into the garage right behind it. He had to act quickly. Soon, everyone would know what he had done.

*   *   *

My phone rang, and I sighed. Reaching into my pocket, I wasn't surprised to see my dad's number on the caller ID. This was his third call in the last hour and a half, which meant I was running dangerously behind schedule. If I didn't leave now, he'd send a search party to my last known location or have officers ping my phone. I typed a quick reply and put my phone away.

"I have to go." I rubbed my eyes and tucked the surveillance photos inside the file.

"Hot date?" Logan Winters asked. The assistant district attorney raised an intrigued eyebrow before checking his watch.

"Dinner with my dad."

"In that case, you better hurry. You don't want to keep Captain DeMarco waiting."

"You do realize he's retired."

"Cops like him never truly retire, Liv." Logan shuffled through the paperwork, sticking a few files inside his messenger bag and the rest in the drawer. "Just make sure you don't tell him I'm the reason you're late."

"Why?" I teased. "Are you afraid of him?"

"Absolutely. By the way, thanks for doing this. I know you've been slammed lately. How are things progressing at the club?"

"It's hard to say, but if something shakes loose, you'll be my first call." I looked down at the photo on his desk. "You'll let me know if anything turns up, right?"

"You'll be my first call," he parroted. "Truly, I appreciate all your help."

"I didn't do anything."

"Let's agree to disagree." Logan opened his office door and pressed against the small of my back as he guided me out of the room. His hand lingered a moment longer than necessary. "Can I offer you a ride?" He palmed his car keys, a fancy fob for a luxury sedan.

"No, but you can validate my parking."

We rode the elevator to the lobby, and he took my parking pass and handed it to someone at reception. He nodded at a harried-looking man who just made it through security. "Hey, Johnny, don't forget we have that pretrial motion due at nine a.m."

"Yeah, yeah, I'm on it." Johnny waved away the warning and gave me the quick once-over. "Detective, anything we can help you with?"

"Not today. I'm off duty."

Logan held out the parking pass to get my attention, even though my eyes constantly roamed my surroundings, taking in every person, exit, and potentially volatile situation, a side effect from too much undercover work. I took the offered pass and pushed through the turnstile.

Once we were outside, I turned to Logan, a new thought forming in my mind. "Do you really think your witness went into hiding?"

"Where else would he be?"

"Lying dead somewhere."

Logan bristled at my comment. He didn't want to think about that possibility. He was still new at the DA's office and determined to do a good job. This was his first big fuckup, and he was worried.

My partner and I gave the DA a slam dunk case, but a key witness vanished before his court appearance. That's why Logan wanted to meet tonight, but rehashing the details of the case and going over the witness's life history and statement proved useless. My gut said it was foul play, but we had no proof.

"I'll find him. He's probably camped out in some

roadside motel."

"Where?" I asked.

"Tahiti, Tijuana, Vegas, El Paso. How should I know? I didn't stash him anywhere."

"Maybe you should have."

"He refused protection, and we had no reason to think he needed it."

"He witnessed a murder."

"Just like most of the witnesses you pass my way." He ran a hand through his hair, clearly frustrated. "If Duncan Crane should have been in protective custody, you people should have put him there."

I gave him a look. "Oh, so now I'm *you people*? When you called three hours ago, you were singing a different tune."

"For fuck's sake, Liv, stop twisting my words. You're the one who started pointing fingers. I'm just saying the police should have taken the first step. That doesn't fall on me. It's not my fault Crane's in the wind." He glanced back at the office building. "And I don't need you accusing me of it."

I eyed him curiously. "I wasn't accusing you of anything."

"Well, it sure sounded like it."

"Guilty conscience?"

His eyes smoldered, and he let out an annoyed growl. Resisting the urge to continue the argument, I turned on my heel. I was already late.

"I'll see you around, Winters."

The drive to my parents' house didn't take long, but I needed to be careful. Even though I didn't plan on taking work home with me, I feared it might follow anyway. So I took the scenic route, adding an extra ten minutes to the commute.

My phone rang again, just as I arrived. Ignoring it, I let myself in and locked the door behind me. "Hey,

Dad," I called.

My greeting was met with the distinctive sound of nails skittering against the tile floor. A brown and black mass raced toward me. I dropped to my knees and held out my arms. Gunnie stood on my thighs and tried to lick my face, his tail wagging a million miles an hour.

"Your doting daughter is finally here. You can call off the search team."

"I was wondering what was taking you so long. I'm starving," Vince DeMarco yelled from the kitchen. "After you get the food in the oven, you can fetch my slippers."

"You must have gotten me confused with your other daughter." I entered the kitchen to find Dad dressed up. "Are we going out to eat?"

"No, I had a meeting at city hall earlier, and then I met some of the guys from the precinct for drinks."

"Uh-huh." I didn't necessarily believe it, but Vince DeMarco could stonewall the best of them. "Where's Mom?"

He chuckled and turned back to chopping vegetables for salad. "She's at her wino meeting."

"You mean book club?"

"That's the story she's sticking with, but you and I know better." He finished making the salad and wiped his hands on a towel before coming around the counter and giving me a hug. "How's work? Did you catch a last minute case?"

"No, I had to go over some things at the DA's office."

"Are you testifying?"

"Not anytime soon."

"Good. It's never a good idea to speak out in open court when you're in the midst of an undercover assignment. UCs should be exempt."

"Well, they do make the occasional exception."

Dad didn't say anything. He put the salad on the table and grabbed the oven mitts. "I heard you put in for a transfer." He took the steaks out of the oven and placed one on each plate, ladling some mushroom sauce over the top. "Anything I should know? Is someone giving you a hard time at the station?"

I went to the sink to wash my hands, buying a few seconds to think. By the time I turned around, Dad had added Brussels sprouts and sweet potato fries to the plates and placed them on the table. He sat down heavily, ignoring Gunnie's big brown eyes which silently begged for scraps.

"Just the usual whispers and cackles." I pulled out my chair and sat down. "My captain used to be your partner, so it comes with the territory. The brass thinks everything I do is amazing and incredible, and everyone else thinks I'm getting special treatment. I don't want it to be like this. I hear the rumors and snickers. I want to do this on my own. To make my own name and my own way."

"Your achievements have nothing to do with me, Olive. You're a good cop. You're smart and dedicated, and the brass noticed. That's how you got where you are."

I cringed at the use of my full first name. My mother must have been out of her mind to name me after a fruit, or she was ordering a martini when the nurse was filling out the paperwork. One or the other. "Yeah, well, tell that to the rumor mill. Making detective at twenty-eight and working in intelligence isn't normal. A lot of the guys think it's favoritism. Sometimes, I'm not sure they're wrong."

Dad cut into his steak and spoke with his mouth full. "It's called hard work."

"If that's true, it won't hurt to move to a new

precinct and start fresh."

He shrugged and continued to eat, but from the silence, I knew he disagreed. However, it was my life. My career. My choice.

Gunnie let out a soft whine, and I slipped the puppy a piece of sweet potato under the table. The furball understood how difficult it was to be a woman in uniform without the added difficulty of having a decorated police captain as your father, or at least that's what those big brown eyes conveyed as he pawed at my leg for a piece of steak.

My phone rang, and I fished it out of my pocket. "Dammit."

"Work?" Dad asked, wiping his hands on a napkin. This had been a constant occurrence growing up, but now it was my turn to answer the siren's song.

"Who else?"

I hit answer, prepared for the worst. Calls after hours usually meant one of two things. Someone was dead, or an op was in trouble. Tonight, it was both.

"We need you at the precinct," Detective Brad Fennel, my partner, said. "Two high-end sports cars just got jacked. We're talking a score of a cool million. The valet was killed, and we're guessing Kincaid's crew is behind it."

"You need help working the scene?" I asked.

"Nah," Brad replied. "We don't want to risk someone making you as a cop. I'll perform the preliminaries and let the techs process the rest. Homicide's here to make sure we don't screw it up, so I'll meet you at the precinct. You're gonna have to get in touch with Axel Kincaid and his boys sooner rather than later. If they get those cars out of the country before we stop them, they'll likely get away with the murder."

"Do we have any evidence?" I asked.

"Just the usual shit."

"So nada."

Brad sighed. "Get down here, Liv. We're on a time crunch."

"I'm on my way." I pushed away from the table and looked at my dad. "I have to go."

"Be careful. And don't forget you're coming to family dinner next week."

"I'll try. Tell Mom I said hi. I'll see you guys soon. I promise." I grabbed my bag and jacket, catching a glimpse of him emptying my plate into Gunnie's bowl.

The puppy wagged his tail and lapped at the mushroom sauce. Apparently, my presence wasn't as coveted as steak scraps. Traitor.

TWO

I read the preliminary reports and reviewed the 911 calls. Since the crime occurred outside a swanky hotel, news reporters were covering the story. I watched the coverage, but, at this point, it was just speculation. We were keeping a lid on the details as best we could. We didn't need the media turning this into a circus.

The police had Axel Kincaid under surveillance, but a few of his crew might have slipped away in order to boost the cars. Over the course of the last three months, my suspicions had grown concerning just how powerful Kincaid really was, but I hadn't said anything to anyone at the station. Perhaps I should have.

Maybe if I did, this wouldn't have happened, but until now, I had no reason to think he was dangerous. Most auto thefts were nonviolent. The parking attendant must have gotten in the way or seen their faces, so they killed him.

I made a few calls and checked with the crime scene team. The stolen cars had GPS trackers and security systems, but they had been deactivated. Whoever took the cars knew exactly what to do to get away with it. Obviously, we were dealing with professionals. That meant they probably had records.

Unfortunately, our prime suspect, Axel Kincaid, was hosting a private event at his club during the time of the murder. The police surveillance unit spotted him entering the club this morning, and he hadn't stepped foot outside since.

Kincaid landed on our radar six months ago when vice got a tip he was running an illegal casino. After several failed attempts to bring Kincaid up on charges that never quite stuck, vice planted several undercovers inside Spark, Kincaid's club. But Kincaid always sniffed them out.

In addition to allegations of a casino, Kincaid had been suspected of several high-end car thefts. It was no secret he traded vehicles in exchange for lost bets or as possible payments. He commanded a fleet. Rumor was he owned a converted warehouse filled with nothing but exotic cars. But winning the vehicles in races or by playing cards wasn't enough for him. Everything he did was about the thrill.

He'd even been brazen enough to joyride past two traffic cops in a hot Maserati. However, the plates were bogus, and with the engine inside that Italian beast, by the time the patrol car caught up to him, he'd already pulled into a warehouse and sealed the doors. He was walking down the block when they stopped him.

The officers detained Kincaid and obtained a warrant. However, when they checked the warehouse, the car was gone. There was no denying Kincaid was the common denominator in these high-end thefts, and the crime today fit Axel's profile perfectly. However, without hard proof, nothing ever stuck.

Kincaid was untouchable. Even I didn't know how he made an Italian sports car vanish into thin air from inside a sealed warehouse. But he did. I was sure of it.

After his little car stunt and vice's failed attempts to infiltrate Kincaid's inner circle, intelligence took over, and I was sent inside. Thus far, Kincaid didn't suspect a thing. I was the only cop who managed to stay off his radar, and every day, I wondered if that was about to change.

He had keen instincts. After all, he survived the streets and emerged victorious. His juvie record indicated a violent, troubled individual with an innate ability to boost cars. By the time he was fifteen, he'd stolen over two million dollars in exotic imports and had been brought up on over half a dozen aggravated assault charges, but as far as society was concerned, it was a phase he outgrew. Now he owned one of the most exclusive clubs in town, catering to the wealthy and enjoying the protection that position afforded him. His clientele boasted the names of some powerful people in government, which is probably how he'd been able to keep his record clean thus far.

Sports cars were his signature item. His commodity of choice. Something he collected and traded like baseball cards. His legal activities only helped to conceal his illegal ones.

I'd only gotten a few glimpses into Spark's private back room, but I'd seen the pink slips and car keys thrown into the pot of several high-stakes poker games. And I heard whispers of specific imports being procured and shipped to overseas buyers. Plus, I overheard some club members talking about Kincaid's races.

Unlike the movies, these cars weren't tricked out pieces of shit driven by teenagers. These vehicles were designed for speed and driven by wealthy thrill-seekers. Six-figure cars raced down the blocked-off streets while people placed bets. It was illegal, not just because of the obvious public endangerment and traffic law violations but also because of the gambling. However, when units rolled up and shut everything down, there was no way to prove Kincaid orchestrated it. He followed the rules of *Fight Club*. And no one was talking, just like tonight.

Even if Kincaid somehow managed to slip out the back, a dozen people would swear he was in the club. And the same would hold true for Axel's top associates. Kincaid's crew always alibied out, and without physical evidence or eyewitness testimony, we were never able to pin anything on them, not even the illicit poker games. But he was guilty as sin. I knew it. We all knew it. We just had no way of proving it.

For the last few months, I'd been working my way into Axel's good graces. A vice informant working as a waitress at Kincaid's club vouched for me when another of his waitresses was arrested for solicitation and possession. Since he was in a bind, he hired me on the spot. And I'd been there ever since.

Most nights, I worked as a waitress. Occasionally, he'd put me in one of the cages to dance. I did whatever he wanted and didn't ask questions. He liked that, almost as much as black leather, a bare midriff, and my fascination with motorcycles. Of course, a woman who enjoyed something powerful between her thighs usually appealed to most men. If they didn't fancy me, they liked the sleek, sporty, Japanese bike my cover persona drove. Too bad motorcycles scared the hell out of me.

I was three months in, but Axel still didn't trust me completely. Trust had to be earned, and he didn't know me well enough to test me. But from the looks he'd given me, it was obvious he wanted to get to know me better. Maybe it was time I took him up on that offer.

"Liv," my partner, Brad Fennel, took a seat at his desk, "are you up to speed?"

"Getting there."

Brad filled me in on the crime, but it was basic. The security footage from the garage showed three masked men inside a white SUV. The SUV followed the valet, who was parking a yellow Ferrari, into the garage. They boxed in the Ferrari. Two of the men stepped out of the car and forced the valet to give up the keys.

For no apparent reason, they shot him three times in the chest. They searched the body, taking the valet's wallet, card case, phone, and a few sets of keys. One of the other sets of keys went to a silver McLaren. The SUV drove away, and the two masked men split up. The security camera didn't catch the SUV's license plate number, but it caught a glimpse of the two sports cars leaving the garage two minutes later.

"Who called it in?" I asked.

"Another valet," Fennel said. "He was parking another car, spotted Juan Rodriguez on the ground, and called 911. By the time first responders arrived, Rodriguez was dead."

"Was Rodriguez still alive when the other valet found him?"

"I don't think so. The ME said he thinks Rodriquez's death was instantaneous." My partner swallowed. He hated bodies. We both did, but he tended to take them more personally than most. I had to do something to get him out of his morbid mood or else he'd find himself at the bottom of a bottle as soon as shift ended.

"Instantaneous, huh? I'm glad that word-a-day calendar is coming in handy, but if you start throwing around big words like that, the other cops are gonna tease you mercilessly." I smirked. "Oh, wait."

He cracked a smile. "You should hear me use apropos in a sentence."

"I just did."

"Shut up." He clicked a few computer keys and focused on me. "What are you thinking?"

"Have you tried pinging Rodriguez's phone? We might be able to track the killer that way."

"No dice. He probably tossed it out the window after they drove away. Have you heard anything coming from Kincaid's crew?"

"Not yet. If Kincaid pulled this off, he must have buyers lined up. I asked cyber division to do some checking. Most deals are brokered online, but since Kincaid's so damn careful, we need to check with our CIs and see if they've heard anything. We should probably read in the auto theft unit and monitor traffic cams. The more eyes, the better."

"Ugh. Are you sure we have to get the state police involved?" Brad mumbled a few derogatory things about incompetent yahoos.

I looked down at my phone. Before Fennel arrived, I made a few calls in between watching the news and reading the reports, but no one bothered to call me back. "We need as many resources on this as possible. We don't want the cars to get loaded into a truck or freight container. You said it yourself; we don't have evidence. So unless we find the cars, or more importantly, the thieves, we have nothing but a body. And I'm sick of people dying for no good reason. Rodriguez is our first DB since we started investigating Kincaid, and if this keeps up, he might not be our last."

Fennel pressed his lips together and assessed me. "I know you, DeMarco. Is this what's got your panties in a twist?"

"Wow, you can tell my panties are twisted from there? Is this why you're a detective? Or are you just hoping I'll flash you to disprove that statement?"

"Seriously, Liv, what's going on? You seem out of sorts."

"We know Axel has a violent past, but this is the first time he's been violent or his crew's been violent. Taking a life jeopardizes everything he's worked to build. Murder can't be swept under the rug as easily as some rich asshole's stolen Porsche. I'm not convinced he's behind this."

"He's the hottest game in town," my partner countered. "He has the connections to move cars like that. If our suspicions are correct, it's how he made his fortune in the first place. And after that Maserati stunt, we know he has the balls."

Regardless, something about the situation didn't feel right. "True, but Kincaid knows this will bring the police knocking. I don't think he'd risk it."

"For a million dollars, I bet he would. Plus, we have nothing to go on. Maybe all the other GTAs were test runs to see how smart we are." Brad eyed me. "We know he's a thrill-seeker. Maybe he just escalated to murder."

"Oh god. I hate to think what that might mean." My phone beeped, and I glanced at the number. It was go-time. I typed out a response and hit send. "Pull the records on every sports car stolen in the last three months. We need to make certain Axel's responsible for all of them." I bit my lip and stared at Brad. "It won't hurt to make sure our assumptions are correct before we rule out other possibilities. I don't want a killer getting away, and I know you don't either."

"You really think another crew is responsible?"

"I don't know. Some of the previous thefts didn't exactly fit Axel's MO, and the timing didn't always coordinate. I've been with him when some of those cars were boosted."

"Yeah, but that doesn't mean he didn't have someone do it for him," Brad argued.

"I don't know. I just don't see how he's moving them without us noticing. We have eyes on his club, his apartment, and the warehouse. Where is he keeping them? Where is he sending them? None of this makes much sense."

"We'll figure it out."

"Yeah."

Fennel sighed and jerked his head at the door. "I'll do some research, but the brass is going to need proof before they scrap this op and start chasing some unknown third party."

"That's why we have to find evidence to prove or disprove my theory."

"Right, because you only follow the evidence."

Unsure if that was a sarcastic remark, I gave my partner a final look and grabbed my phone. It was time I went back into the trenches.

THREE

He was jittery. He didn't expect to be. He thought he would be calm and relaxed now that it was done. But instead, he was wired. It must be the adrenaline. He felt more alive than ever before, but the feeling was fading fast. It was like a drug, and he already wanted another hit.

Steady, he thought. He closed his eyes and leaned into the headrest. He could still feel the vibration of the engine coursing through him. His hands tingled. The friction from his sleek leather driving gloves caressing the steering wheel usually sent a pleasant jolt through him, but this time, it was the jerk of the forty caliber he remembered. That was unexpected but necessary.

He recalled the look on Juan Rodriguez's face the moment the bullet pierced his heart. The parking attendant shouldn't have turned around. He should have taken the path to the walkway, like he always did, and returned to the valet stand. Instead, Juan turned around and recognized the white SUV. It was that moment which sealed his fate.

Despite the mask, Juan could identify him. And that posed a problem. So he fixed it. Three shots. That's all it took. The force of the blast knocked Juan to the ground. The blood sprayed backward and forward, misting the side of the white SUV and leaving a thick, runny ketchup-like stain against the shiny yellow sports car.

The boom had been so loud. It practically echoed. He chuckled, realizing in the utter silence that he still heard a distinct ringing in his ears from the weapon being discharged in an enclosed space. Next time, he'd wear earplugs. He didn't want any of his senses deadened, but he didn't want to risk permanent hearing loss. He lived on the edge and wanted to experience everything. He wouldn't be able to do that with a blown-out eardrum. He'd have to be more careful in the future.

Lights flashed twice behind him, and he checked the rearview mirror. It was safe. He brushed his hand over the steering wheel one last time, tracing the symbol. He'd never see the car again. He tucked the gun away and climbed out. The car would be scrubbed. The evidence eradicated. The police would come looking, but they'd never find anything. He was confident. He had the perfect plan. He would enjoy watching them frantically search. The police would never stop hunting, but he wasn't afraid. He was amused.

*   *   *

After a quick detour to my cover apartment to change clothes, put on my makeup, and exchange my car for the motorcycle, I went to Spark, Axel Kincaid's club. The side entrance required client verification, and I waved at the security camera aimed at my face.

"Hey, buzz me in. I left my wallet in my locker last night." In actuality, I left the wallet with my cover ID and fake credit cards inside the locker most nights in case Axel ever wanted to make sure I was who I claimed to be. "George, c'mon, don't be a buster." I tapped my foot impatiently and made a face. "Fine, but I'm going to tell Mr. Kincaid you wouldn't let me in."

I pulled out my phone and dialed Axel's office line. He was too careful to give me his actual cell number, but I knew he had the calls forwarded. I waited, listening to the ringing, but he wasn't answering.

Of course, you can't answer your phone. You're not here, I thought. It went to voicemail, and I hung up and tried again. I stared up at the camera. "Come on. Let me in. Please."

"Hey," Axel said, surprising me, "what's wrong?"

"George won't let me inside."

"George isn't working tonight. No one is. The club's closed."

"Why?"

"What do you want, Liv?"

"I think I left my wallet in my locker. I was going to grab a drink, but I don't have my ID."

"Go to Serano's. They don't card."

"Can't you just let me in?"

"I'm hosting a private function. I'll see you tomorrow." He hung up, and I let out a frustrated sigh.

A private function. Based on the nearby cars and the low rumble coming from within the building, people were definitely inside, but I was having a difficult time believing Axel was. His lack of appearance was practically a confession, except the courts would never see it that way. And even if he wasn't involved in the two recent thefts and the murder, whatever was going on inside Spark right now had to be illegal. I just didn't know what it was, and without a warrant, I'd never find out. Or would I?

I returned to my bike and sent a text to my CI. We needed to meet. Twenty minutes later, I pulled up to a dive bar on Amsterdam. The regulars clustered around the TVs, nursing hangovers or what would eventually become hangovers. Rebecca or Becca, as she was better known, flicked her gaze to the smoke-filled rear of the bar where a few of Axel's crew were shooting pool. The only time they ever ventured off their home turf was when Axel closed the club early. At least Kincaid's story tracked.

I ordered sparkling water and glanced at the boys. Fox and Emilio acted like they hadn't seen me, but I wasn't convinced. Their presence here meant trouble.

Taking the glass, I slid into the cracked vinyl booth across from Becca. Her right leg jittered up and down. She took a deep drink from her glass and rubbed at her running mascara. Her left eye had a new bruise, but I didn't comment. She kept one hand on the glass. The other she used to wipe her constantly running nose. She had all the telltale markings of an addict, including the career as a pro to go with it.

"Hey," I said, keeping one eye on the guys, "how long have you been here?"

"Not long."

"What about them?"

She shrugged. "Don't know. They were here when I arrived."

"How 'bout you finish that and we'll take a walk? It's a little too crowded in here."

"Yeah, okay." She tipped back the glass, downing whatever was left in a single gulp.

I placed my water on another table as I followed her out of the bar. I felt their eyes on us. Emilio might not care what I was doing here, but Fox would be curious. I'd have to come up with a decent excuse, but that could wait.

We didn't speak until we were a block and a half from the bar. We ducked down a tiny dead end alley with ample streetlights. It was one of Becca's favorites to work because the light kept away a certain level of depravity. It made her feel safe.

"Am I getting paid?" she asked, leaning against a wall while she pulled a pack of cigarettes and a lighter from the top of her thigh-high boot.

"You know I always deliver." I pulled an envelope from the inside of my jacket and held it up. She trusted me enough not to ask to count it. She reached for it, but I tucked it back into my jacket. "Intel first. Are you working tonight?"

"I'm always working." She puffed out a plume of smoke. "What can I do for you, Detective?"

"What do you know about the recent string of GTAs?"

"Cars get taken all the time. Doesn't mean I know a thing about it."

"I'm not talking about just any cars. I'm talking about two very specific cars. High-end, custom jobs. A Ferrari and a McLaren. Ring any bells?"

"Nope." She took another drag of her cigarette.

The red lipstick smudge on the paper caught my eye, and I wondered briefly if she could be playing me. Axel's guys were at the same bar where we planned to meet. Becca could have tipped them that I was a cop. The uneasiness wormed its way through my belly, but I forced myself not to jump to conclusions.

"Who roughed you up?" I asked.

She snorted. "Some john."

"Yeah," I looked toward the street, "want me to take care of that for you?"

"Let it go."

"It wasn't Fox or Emilio, was it?"

"Shit." She gave me a look. "I'm not an idiot. I wouldn't sell you out. I don't hang with their crew, and you know it."

I didn't necessarily believe that, but she was three seconds away from shutting down. And I needed a lead. "Good. I just wanted to make sure you were still into our arrangement."

In response, she blew a puff of smoke in my face. "Just waiting on the cash."

"You gotta earn it."

She didn't volunteer any information, so I tried again.

"Since you're always working, you know the streets. You hear things. See things. You normally work outside Spark, making easy cash when the drunks stumble out."

"So?"

"Did anyone mention what kind of event Axel's hosting tonight?"

"I don't know."

"Does it have anything to do with cars?"

She dropped the cigarette butt to the ground and snubbed it out with her boot. "Everything with him is fast rides." She smiled wickedly. "But that doesn't always mean cars." She knew a secret and had no intention of sharing it. She eyed me up and down. "I'm surprised he hasn't tried to turn you out yet. Maybe he can smell that cop stink on you."

"Is he running girls?"

She lit another cigarette. "I wouldn't be surprised. Word on the street is, whatever you want, he can get. It's about the experience. You bring enough cash, you can snort a few lines, race down the coast, and get blown all at the same time."

"Where does he get the cars?"

"Damn, you're obsessed. Why the fascination?" Becca was enjoying toying with me.

"Stop playing games and tell me what you know about the cars," I snapped.

She bounced from leg to leg, getting antsy again. "The only time I'm ever inside a fancy ride is when I'm kneeling in the front seat."

"Was that story about the blow and being blown what actually happened? Did Kincaid pimp you out to one of his clients?"

"Even if that did happen, it'd be the word of a whore against the denial of a judge. So no, it didn't happen." She crushed the second cigarette butt into the pavement. "You need to stop worrying about the cars and think about what's going on inside them."

"Which is?"

She shrugged. "I don't know, and that's the truth."

"Fine. Any idea why Fox and Emilio just happened to show up at this particular bar tonight?"

"Why don't you ask them?"

I turned to leave.

"Liv," she whined, "what about my money?"

"You didn't tell me anything I didn't already know."

Her fake nails clawed at my shoulder, and I spun around to face her. "Axel is in this for the thrills. Cars. No cars. It doesn't matter. The danger gets him off. His clients are the same way. He understands their desires and capitalizes on them. He likes to call it the Vegas experience. What happens in Vegas, stays in Vegas."

"I need to know where he's been for the last few hours."

She flinched, casting her gaze to the sidewalk. "I can't help you with that."

"Someone got killed. Do you think he'd cross that

line?"

"Who?" The disbelief shone in her eyes.

"A parking attendant."

She swallowed. "Axel and his crew don't pop people without provocation. Assuming this has to do with the cars you keep harping on, I'd say you're barking up the wrong tree. You need to leave this alone. I bet those pricks can afford new rides anyway."

I looked at her. She knew a lot more than she was letting on. "Who would do something like this?"

"I'll ask around, but I can't make no promises. And you owe me."

I pulled out the envelope and peeled off a stack of twenties. "Half now. The rest when you get a name. Text me when you know something."

"Yep."

I gave her one last look. "Stay safe." I gestured at her eye. "You need help, there's an ER nurse, Emma, she'll take care of you. Remember that, okay?"

"Yeah."

Without anything solid to work with, I headed back to the bar, but before I could get more than a few feet away, Becca cleared her throat.

"Be mindful of the company you keep. You know what they say about lying down with dogs."

"Does someone have a bone to pick with me?" I inquired, turning and walking backward, still intent on my destination.

"Just be careful out there. These streets aren't safe for a tasty thing like you."

As I trudged back to the bar, I couldn't help but think they weren't safe for anyone.

FOUR

I ordered a beer and took a seat in the corner. Emilio spotted me and jerked his chin up in greeting. I returned the gesture and waited. After they finished their game, he and Fox sauntered over to my corner of the bar. Emilio sat beside me, but Fox remained standing.

"What's going on at Spark?" I asked. "The place looked shut down. I was forced to come here. Apparently, so were you two."

"Axel closed up early," Fox said. "Family emergency."

"I thought you guys were his family."

Emilio shrugged and gestured to the bartender who filled a few shots and put them on the bar in front of us. "Drink up, chica. It's on me."

"Thanks." I tossed one back. Drinking on the job wasn't exactly SOP, but as a UC, I had special clearance. However, this was the last thing I wanted to be doing right now.

Emilio put his hand on my stool and dragged me

closer to him. He put his arm around my waist and rubbed his thumb against my thigh. "I saw you leave with that whore a few minutes ago."

"You got something against whores?" I asked.

"If he did, he'd have to stop talking to his mama," Fox quipped. He ignored Emilio's protests. His razor-sharp gaze remained focused on me. "You turning tricks too?"

"Not exactly."

"What exactly?" Fox leaned across the bar, effectively pinning me between him and Emilio.

"Dude," I gave him a look, "are you shitting me right now?"

"Answer the question."

I let out an exaggerated huff and slowly reached into my jacket for the envelope of cash. "I had something she needed."

He thumbed through the cash. "You dealing?"

"Hey, I can't help it if some Wall Street guy left an eight ball as a tip." I snickered and stuffed the envelope back into my jacket. "Actually, you wouldn't believe how many times that happens."

"I know," Emilio said, earning himself a searing look from Fox.

"Anyway, I'm not much of a partier, but I could use a few extra bucks. Becca is a friend of a friend, so I hook her up from time to time." I narrowed my eyes. "Am I stepping on your toes? I didn't realize this was your turf."

Fox straightened. "Does Axel know about this?"

"What?"

"That someone's bringing drugs into the club?"

"I don't know."

"The next time it happens, you better notify security."

"Yeah, okay." I blinked. "Am I in trouble?"

Fox narrowed his eyes, growing bored with me and the conversation. "That's not up to me."

"Leave her alone," Emilio said. "She didn't bring them into Spark. She just moved them out of there." Fox gave him an intense look, but Emilio ignored it and pawed at my leg more enthusiastically than Gunnie begging for scraps. "Olivia's clean. She's not like Candi."

Fox ignored us and ordered another drink.

As usual, I let Axel's guys hang all over me. So far, no one had tried to cross the line, but I had a feeling it was because Axel kept them in check. Tonight, he wasn't around, and I wondered how far things would progress.

Since Emilio was buying, Fox ordered more shots, and I kept sliding the glasses over to Emilio, who had no problem putting one away after another. I let my head rest on his shoulder in a friendly, familiar gesture. These were my people too. I was one of them. At least, I hoped they believed it.

An uneasy twinge remained in my gut. I should be doing something useful, and tonight, I hadn't gotten even the slightest bit of usable intel from my CI or the two members of Axel's crew. Frankly, I still wasn't certain I hadn't been made. And that worried me.

Fox's phone buzzed, and I glanced at him from the corner of my eye. He was too focused on replying to notice I was paying attention. If I squinted, I could make out two of the words. *Deal's done.* Clumsily, I reached across the bar for a napkin, bumping a cup with ice and knocking it over.

"I'm sorry." I reached for more napkins.

Fox put his phone on top of the bar and grabbed the now empty glass, shoving the dropped cubes back inside while I wiped up the water with a napkin. My eyes went to his phone's screen. *Five cars.*

Five? We only knew about two.

Fox saw me looking at his phone and put it in his pocket.

"Did it get wet?" I asked.

"It's fine." He glared at Emilio who was humming to himself. Whenever he got really drunk, he'd sing in Spanish. Based on the level of his humming, he was one drink away from impersonating Enrique Iglesias. "Yo," he said, peeling Emilio's arm off my leg, "we gotta go."

"Huh?" Emilio asked. He blinked a few times and looked around. "Yeah, okay." He gave my cheek a sloppy kiss. "See you tomorrow at Spark."

"You can count on it." My eyes met Fox's. "Sorry about your phone."

He grunted and dragged Emilio out of the bar. I remained where I was, using the mirrors to make sure they left. Then I ordered a club soda and studied the regulars. No one stood out, and I didn't see any other members of Axel's crew anywhere.

When I finished my soda, I grabbed my purse and went into the ladies' room. For a dive bar, it actually had a large bathroom. The door swung shut, and I checked underneath the stalls to make sure the room was empty. I wiped off the counter and put my purse down.

Five cars. Was that their endgame? Or was that the number of high-end rides they'd already boosted? I'd have to do some more asking but not tonight. I was out of contacts and luck.

I sent a text to Brad. The police needed to be aware three more thefts were imminent. Hopefully, we already filled our quota for murder this evening. I didn't think Brad or I could take another loss, especially when my entire assignment was intended to prevent such things from happening.

Get back here if you can, Brad replied.

I told him I was on my way and slipped out of the restroom. No one noticed when I left the bar or walked a block to my bike. After returning to my cover apartment, I traded my bike for a late model sedan and checked my mirrors. No one was around. It was nearly midnight, and the streets were practically empty. Still, I was careful and meandered aimlessly, checking for tails.

When I was sure it was safe, I headed for the station, but I couldn't help but notice the one glaringly obvious discrepancy. Becca said Axel's crew wasn't involved in the murder or the recent thefts, but Fox's phone said otherwise.

Inevitably, this investigation would have to be left to the men in uniform. I couldn't risk blowing my cover, and until I was positive Axel's inner circle was involved, we couldn't rule out other possibilities. Whoever did this was ballsy and stupid. And I just spent the last two hours in a bar with Ballsy and Stupid.

FIVE

He watched her leave the bar. She was careful. She looked around, practically jumping at shadows. He admired the tight leather pants she wore and the way they accentuated the curve of her ass. The leather jacket and crop top were a nice touch. The silky skin of her bared stomach glowed in the streetlight just before she zipped the jacket and reached for her helmet.

She had no idea he was watching her tonight, unlike most nights where he ogled her without hesitation as she moved through Spark or remained locked in a cage. She'd smile at him on occasion and ask if he needed anything. She was clueless, which made it all the more entertaining for him since he knew exactly who she was and why she was there.

You can't fool me, Detective DeMarco, he thought. Truth be told, he liked her best in the cage. On those nights, he'd smile back, wondering if she realized she was trapped.

He could end this now. Make it look like an

accident. No one else knew she was a cop or knew of the investigation. But he did. He knew the real reason she met with the traitorous whore. She wanted information on him. But she wouldn't get it. He'd make sure of that.

The motorcycle sped off in the direction of her apartment, and he turned the key in the ignition. There was no need to rush. He knew where she was going.

He arrived several minutes after she did and found a parking space a few blocks away and waited to see what she'd do now. Maybe she'd give up. It was late. Perhaps she'd call it quits for the night.

He could probably sneak upstairs and knock on her door. When she answered, he would kill her. But that would end the game too quickly. He exhaled, replaying the memory from earlier. He could still feel the weight of the gun in his hand. The sound of the blast. The blood blossoming.

His gaze went to the center console. He should lose the gun. He already unloaded the cars, preparing them for shipment. But it served as a reminder, a way to relive those few, precious moments. He'd dump it in a few days. Keeping it posed a danger, which excited him, but it was more a perceived risk than an actual risk since the police were clueless. It wasn't a real concern, which meant he could revel in the memory a little while longer.

A minute later, DeMarco left the apartment building and performed another visual sweep before setting off in the opposite direction, toward the sedan she parked a few streets over. He blew out a breath and watched as she started the car. He'd bide his time and see where the investigation led before deciding if he needed to strike.

*　　*　　*

"Earth to DeMarco," my partner waved the USB in front of my face, "I got the security footage from the hotel."

"Thanks." I raised an eyebrow at him. "Do you want to save me some time and tell me what's on it?"

"You were right. The white SUV was staking out the place. Whoever killed the parking attendant planned every move."

"Do you think the murder was premeditated?"

Fennel bit his lip. "I don't know."

"That should be our new catchphrase."

"I was hoping for 'gotcha suckas,' but we'll keep it in mind." He tossed the USB to me. "Premeditated would mean Mr. Rodriguez was the target, not the Ferrari or the McLaren. I'm not sure that tracks."

I clicked a few keys and rubbed my eyes, wiping the greasy smear of eyeliner off my fingertips and onto my jeans. By now, I should be used to the clown makeup, but I wasn't. Normally, I would have changed before coming to work, but I didn't want to waste time when another heist might be imminent. It was bad enough I spent an extra thirty minutes driving in circles.

"Rodriguez is clean. No criminal record. No outstanding debt." I scrolled through the details. "Has next of kin been notified?"

"His family lives in Florida. They're catching a flight in the morning."

"What about his apartment?"

"Uniforms went to check it out. Rodriguez lived alone. Nothing inside indicated he had enemies, but uniforms are performing a canvass just to make sure we aren't missing something." I opened my mouth to ask another question, and Brad narrowed his eyes at me. "Save your breath. His coworkers don't know anything either."

"About why someone would want to kill him or about the recent string of GTAs?"

"Either." He grabbed a tissue and handed it to me. "You look like a raccoon."

"Don't you like raccoons?"

"The notorious burglars of the animal kingdom? Not really."

"Damn, that's another big word." I dabbed at my eyes, catching his amused smile.

"You know, you don't have to do that. I'm okay," he insisted.

"You sure?"

He nodded tightly, his gaze shifting around the room to make sure no one was paying attention. "You don't have to keep me entertained or distracted. I'm not going to fall down the rabbit hole, at least not tonight."

"Maybe I just like busting your balls. I barely get to see you anymore, so I have to condense my jabs when I get the chance." I winked. "That's what partners are for."

"Just remember, payback's a bitch."

His words triggered a thought, and I clicked a few more keys. "Brad, you're a genius."

"So I've been told." He leaned back in his chair. "What did you find?"

"I'm not sure."

"No wonder we're partnered together. They needed my brain to make up for your lack of smarts."

"That must mean I'm the good-looking one."

"I'm not saying a word. That's an HR nightmare waiting to happen."

"Damn, you really are the brains of this operation."

He came around the desk to see what I was doing. "You think the owners were targeted rather than the vehicles?"

"Becca said they could afford new rides. It might have been an off the cuff comment, but I don't know." I continued searching news articles and social media for anyone who might hold a grudge against the car owners.

Since the owners were wealthy tycoons with companies and foundations which controlled a good portion of buildings and businesses in the city, it didn't seem that farfetched. Then again, killing a working-class guy while stealing fancy cars didn't exactly jibe with that theory.

"Did the killer steal anything else from Mr. Rodriguez besides his wallet, cell phone, and car keys?" I asked, my eyes never leaving the screen.

"The techs made a list of items based on the footage from the security feed. Let me grab it." Brad returned a second later. "Four sets of keys. A cell phone. Wallet. And a black card case."

Brad plugged the USB into his computer while I scribbled down a list of potential grudge-holders we needed to question. He paused the screen, and we switched places. I stared at the monitor, seeing the pool of blood beneath the body. Closing my eyes, I said a silent prayer this wouldn't happen again.

Filled with a newfound resolve, I zoomed in and stared at the item. "I don't think that's a case. It's too flat. It looks like a card. Maybe a keycard."

"To what?"

"I don't know. Check with the hotel."

"Already on it." When Brad hung up the phone, he smiled. "You were right. Some hotel staff are issued master keycards for the hotel entrances and maintenance facilities. They're solid black, and it isn't listed in the items we recovered. The killer took it."

"He must have had a reason." I just didn't know

what it was.

"It looks like a mugging. Maybe he thought it was a credit card or a card case, like we initially believed."

"Or he knew exactly what it was and has other plans in mind."

I closed my eyes and tried to clear the million thoughts racing through my brain. *Five cars.* That's what the text on Fox's phone said.

"Were the owners staying at the hotel?" I asked, frantically flipping pages and getting annoyed because Fennel kept his desk alphabetized instead of stacked in the order information came in. "How do you find anything?"

"Get up."

We switched desks, and I continued perusing the webpages I had read earlier. The car owners lived locally but were at the hotel to attend a charity function. The hotel didn't have a room reservation for Mr. Stevens, but they did have a reservation for Mr. Hart. Nixing the theory that the murderous car thief planned to sneak inside the hotel and retarget Hart and Stevens, I went back to researching possible enemies the two men had in common.

"Has anyone spoken to Hart or Stevens yet?" I asked.

"Briefly. They're coming in tomorrow afternoon to give official statements."

"We don't have time for this." I swore. "Where are we on traffic cam footage? Any sightings?"

"The department set up a tip line. We issued a statement during the eleven o'clock news." He rubbed a hand over his mouth and blew out a breath. "Look, we'll figure it out, but it's late. There's nothing left for us to do tonight. Go home. Get some sleep, and we'll start fresh in the morning."

"The hell with that."

"Liv," he gave me a look, "it's after midnight. The techs have done what they can. We have a ton of interviews lined up tomorrow. We'll leave the rest to the boys who just got on shift." He jerked his chin at the captain's darkened office. "He ordered me to go home hours ago, and unlike you, I'm not Teflon. I don't want my ass chewed in the morning."

I scratched my eyebrow and logged off the computer. "Yeah, okay."

He put on his jacket and turned off his monitor. "I'll walk you out."

"Actually, I'm going to wash up first. You go on ahead."

"Are you staying at the cover apartment?"

"Might as well. Kincaid's boys probably know where I live, so I gotta make it look good. Who knows, maybe one of them will come knocking."

He stared into my eyes. "You need me, I'm there."

"Let's hope that's not the case." I gave him a small smile. "But if I do call, will you be sober enough to drive?"

"For you, anything." He clapped my shoulder and headed for the stairs.

I watched him leave, and then I dug through my desk drawer. After finding my toiletry kit, I went down to the locker rooms, washed the gunk off my face, and changed clothes. For a moment, I stared at my reflection in the mirror. A soul left this earth tonight, and I had no idea who was responsible. But I would find out.

SIX

"You're in early," Brad said, and I jerked upright. "Jesus. I didn't mean to startle you." He put the second cup of coffee down on my desk and took a seat. "You look like hell."

I struggled to straighten my neck. "Nothing an hour of hot yoga or a full body massage won't fix."

"Don't tell me you stayed here all night."

"Okay."

"But you did." He glanced into the captain's office. "Did you get any kind of blowback?"

I shook my head.

Officer Roberts overheard our conversation and snickered, exchanging jokes with three nearby uniforms. My jaw muscles clenched, but I resisted the urge to turn around and say something. It was easier to pretend I didn't hear it, but my partner heard it.

"Show some respect, Officer," Fennel ordered. He moved to get up, and I put my hand on his arm to stop him. It wasn't worth it, at least not at this particular moment.

"Yes, sir," Roberts said. The group moved away, and I sighed.

"Asshole," Fennel muttered. "You can't let them get away with that."

"We've talked about this before," I reminded him. Before I could say anything else, my desk phone rang. "Detective DeMarco," I answered.

After Fennel left last night, the phone never stopped ringing. The tip line was surging with useless intel. Apparently, half the city thought they spotted at least one of the cars and wanted to know if there was a reward. So far, every single call had been a bust.

"Damn, I misdialed. I was thinking about a brilliant brunette I know and must have called you instead," Logan Winters teased. It was a joke meant to rile my feathers, but he couldn't bait me. The assistant district attorney liked to flirt, but it never went beyond a few words here and there. He thought he was charming. I thought he was desperate.

"Well, hang up and try your call again."

He laughed. "I wanted to apologize for our little tiff and was wondering if you could stop by later."

"Probably not. I'm in the middle of an investigation. Is it pressing?"

"It's about our missing witness."

"Did you find him?"

"Not yet. I had a thought and could use your help."

I blew out a breath. I had to focus on my case. Finding the witness would have to wait. "I'll call you as soon as I have some time."

"You're sure you won't be free later?" He sounded hopeful. "I'll buy dinner."

"Sorry, in the event I have some spare time, I'll be manning the tip line and fielding calls from perverts."

"In that case, I should ask what you're wearing."

"Four layers of sweaters under a big puffy ski coat."

"You're such a buzzkill." He let out a long exhale. "The judge granted a continuance, but if I can't put Crane on the stand, the case will get kicked. We have to figure something out. We can't let a killer go free, but I guess that's up to me. You catch them, and I make sure they stay caught."

"That sounds about right." And now I felt guilty and responsible. "As soon as I get a handle on this current situation, I'll do whatever I can to help you locate Crane. Okay?"

"Good luck, Liv." He hung up, and I put the phone back in its cradle.

"DeMarco, Fennel," the captain called from his office, "get in here."

My partner and I exchanged a glance and stepped into Captain Grayson's office. As predicted, he wanted an update on the situation. He sat with his fingers steepled, absently tapping them against his chin as we spoke. When I was finished telling him my theories on Kincaid and his crew, my interaction with Becca, and the texts on Fox's phone, my partner took over the briefing.

The captain swiveled in his chair. "Do you have the vehicle information?" Fennel handed it to him, and Grayson skimmed the details. "Anything else that might be useful?"

"Not that we're aware." I glanced at Brad to make sure we were in agreement.

The captain sighed. "I just got a call. Three more cars were reported stolen. They weren't as high-end as these," he flicked the file, "but they could be part of the five, assuming the text message was accurate."

"Was anyone hurt?" I asked.

Grayson shook his head. "We don't even know exactly when the cars went missing. They were reported stolen this morning. The victims are being questioned now, and I have people checking nearby traffic cams to see if we can pinpoint when it happened. Our surveillance team said Kincaid never left the club last night."

"He keeps an apartment above Spark," I said.

Grayson nodded. "Even if Kincaid isn't directly involved, his crew might be. And we can't account for their whereabouts."

"Unfortunately, Fox and Emilio have an alibi until around midnight," I said.

"See what you can dig up on the rest." Grayson nodded at the door, and Brad and I filed out.

Fennel checked the time. Juan Rodriguez's family should be arriving any minute. Mr. Stevens and Mr. Hart made appointments around lunchtime, using the excuse they were busy men. They probably didn't even care their cars were stolen. It was just like Becca said; they could afford to buy new ones, even without their insurance payouts.

Going to the computer, I researched stolen vehicles. Since Captain Grayson just heard the news, I wasn't sure if the crimes had been logged yet. After refreshing the page a few times, I found them. Two luxury sedans and an SUV had been stolen. I printed the vehicle registration information and opened another database, hoping to find a connection between those three thefts and the two from yesterday, while Brad continued to search for any ties between the victims.

"Did you have time to look into the previous thefts like I asked?"

Brad nodded, but his eyes remained on the computer screen. "Seven luxury imports have been stolen in the last three months. Kincaid has an airtight alibi for two of the thefts but not the others. I asked around and dug through the reports, but as far as I can tell, no other thief operating in the area has the skills needed to get away with stealing cars like that. If it happened once, I'd say it was a fluke. But not seven times."

"So it has to be Axel or someone he trained." My thoughts went to Fox and Emilio. "We need to figure out if Stevens or Hart has any connection to Axel." Given their financial portfolios, I had a feeling they might be members of Spark. But before I got sidetracked, I needed to find out more about the other three cars that were stolen during the night.

I found the service history on the vehicles and hoped something important would turn up. "Hey," I held out the owners' names, "run those and see what you find."

"Sure." Fennel did some quick typing. "Stacy Smith owns one of the sedans and has a dozen different traffic violations, and Ryan Hodges was involved in a fender bender. But neither of those incidents link to Hart or Stevens or the thief. The SUV is registered to a company that provides car service specifically to and from the airport. As far as I can tell, the victims don't have any common enemies."

"Hey, look what I found." I spun my monitor around so Brad could see it and hit play. DOT footage showed a tow truck loading the SUV onto the bed and driving away. We watched the footage a few more times for any indication of who the driver might be. "Can you make out a plate?" I asked.

Brad squinted. "I don't think there is one." He grabbed his phone and requested additional information from nearby cameras. "Freeze it there." He pointed to the screen. "At least we have a name." Towers Wrecker Service.

I pulled up a business profile, but Towers Wrecker went out of business five years ago. "Dammit." I slammed my palm on the desk. Maybe we could figure out who bought the tow truck when the business went under, but it would take time, just like everything else.

"I'll get someone to pull titles and ownership records." My partner placed the request and looked at me. "I've been meaning to ask why you and ADA Winters are so buddy-buddy lately. Are you getting tired of slumming it at the precinct? Or did he finally grow a pair and ask you out?"

"He asked if I could help him locate Crane. He has a few theories where Crane might have gone, but they've turned into dead ends." I glanced at the phone. "Winters might have come up with something else to try, but it can wait." I gave Brad a sideways look. "You think he likes me?"

My partner chuckled. "Do you want me to pass him a note during study hall and find out?"

"Ha ha. Get back to work."

An officer nodded to Brad, and he swallowed. "Speaking of which, it's showtime." He slipped his jacket on and tidied his appearance. This was always the worst part of the job.

I pushed away from the desk just as the phone rang again. "DeMarco," I said, surprised to hear my best friend's voice.

"Liv," Emma said, "a woman was just brought in. No ID, but she had your card in her boot."

"Shit." I rubbed my eyes. "What does she look like?"

"A street-walker who got caught in a meat grinder. You need to get down here," Emma insisted.

Brad looked at me. "Take care of that. I'll handle this." He disappeared into the conference room, and I grabbed my bag.

Expecting the worst, I drove straight to the hospital. My stomach twisted in knots. My gut knew what I'd find, but I hoped I was wrong. A dozen working girls had been given my card at one point or another. It could be anyone. It didn't have to be Becca.

"Liv," Emma called the moment I stepped into the ER. She waved me over to patient intake and buzzed me through the door, saving me the trouble of flashing my badge. "Hey, girl." She hugged me. "It's so good to see you. It's been weeks. I wish it wasn't under these circumstances, though."

"Yeah, me too." I glanced around. "Where's the patient?"

"She just got out of surgery. Broken jaw, cracked ribs, a skull fracture, and a shattered ulna. She's going to be out a while. The docs haven't ruled out brain damage, but they can't say for sure."

"Who is she?"

"I don't know. We called it in. Some rookie is still filling out the paperwork. He ran her prints, but he never gave us a name."

I rolled my eyes. The police department was always stretched too thin. "Let me see her."

Emma led the way to recovery. She pointed at a door, and I peered in the window. Even though it looked like her face went through a wood chipper, it was Becca.

"Her name's Rebecca Johnson." I sunk against the wall, pressing the heels of my hands into my eyes. "Did she have any cash on her?"

"No." Emma crouched in front of me. "Whoever did this took everything, except your card."

"It's called sending a message." I took a deep breath and straightened. "How did she get here?"

"I think someone dropped her off."

"Point me in the direction of the responding officer, and I'll take it from there."

Emma gave me a look. "Are you okay?"

"I'll let you know after I find the animal who did this."

SEVEN

He took a sip of his coffee and watched the detective walk through the automatic doors. She moved with a stiff gait, her pallor a sickly pale. After she tucked the phone away, she stopped near a trashcan and heaved, her body jerking violently. She wiped her mouth and straightened, a newfound determination in her eyes.

A frown tugged at his lips, and he put the coffee down, studying the blisters on his fingers from the crowbar. Feeling the stiffness from the repeated hits, he rotated his shoulder. He hadn't slept in a day and a half, and the fatigue was starting to wear on him. He couldn't remember how many times he struck the whore. It was all a blur.

He nearly lost control, but he stopped himself, remembering she needed to be taught a lesson. Talking to the police was not acceptable. The only reason he drove her to the hospital was to make sure the police discovered what he'd done, but now he had to scrap another car. At least he was smart enough to use the SUV from the heist. It made one less he'd have to part with.

He sighed, rethinking his actions. Maybe he should have killed Becca. The only reason he didn't was because he wanted to send a message to the detective, but from the look on Liv's face, she was too dense to understand. He would make her understand. He would make the entire force understand. If they continued to fuck with his operation, he would fuck with them. At least the assault would keep the detective distracted and off-kilter. He couldn't afford for her to realize what was going on.

He pulled out of the parking lot before she even made it back to her car. First, he would lose the SUV. Then, he'd get some sleep. He had a big night planned.

*   *   *

After leaving the hospital, I went back to the precinct and updated Captain Grayson on the situation. Matters were escalating. We had to get on top of this. Even though I was a cop, trained to gather evidence, work out new leads, and spend countless hours performing computer searches and follow-ups with witnesses, my partner would have to handle most of it on his own. Since I was the only one who had access to Axel Kincaid and his crew, I had to find out what they knew.

Fox and Emilio saw me with Becca last night. They left before I did. Maybe they found her and asked what we really talked about. Maybe they nearly beat her to death because they believed she found another dealer to feed her addiction. Either way, they were my best bet. And as soon as I could place them in her vicinity, we would bring them in. Maybe we'd even get enough for a warrant, and then we could see exactly who texted Fox and what those messages said. It was a lot of ifs, and I didn't hold out much hope.

"Hey," Brad grabbed my arm just as I made it to the stairwell, "we spotted the same white SUV from the hotel parking garage dumping Ms. Johnson outside the ER. We still didn't get a plate, but techs are working on enhancing the image. Hopefully, we'll be able to ID the driver."

"At least we know we're on the right track. I just wish Becca told me what she knew. If she…" My throat tightened. "Maybe I pushed too hard."

"She's your CI. She knew the risks. And I know you. You didn't make her do anything she didn't want to."

"Didn't I?" Another wave of guilt washed over me.

"It's not your fault, Liv." He squeezed my arm, the compassion eking from his eyes. "Grayson's keeping a team on standby. We'll do our best to keep you in our sights without compromising your cover, but you need to be careful out there. These are dangerous stakes." His light brown eyes stared into mine. "If you have to break cover, do it. We're not just dealing with car thieves. We're dealing with a sadist who's already killed once. He won't hesitate to do it again."

"Newsflash, Fennel, we trained for this. Remember? Plus, the doctors don't know if Becca will make it. We might already be looking at two murders."

"Yeah, well, we won't let him get to three." Someone called to Brad from the bullpen, and he turned to acknowledge them. "I'll drop by later to fix your fridge or install your cable or whatever the captain comes up with. We don't want to leave you alone and vulnerable."

"Too bad. I'm the only one invited into the lion's den. And since Becca had my card, he knows we're on to him. I just don't know if I've been blown."

"As soon as we get verification Mr. Hart and Mr. Stevens are members of Spark, we'll bring Axel in for questioning." He handed me a switchblade. It was against department policy, and I gave him a confused look. "Support will be a minute out, but a lot can happen in a minute. Don't take any chances, partner."

He turned to leave, and I called after him, "If I find you in my apartment, you better have dinner on the table."

"Fine, but first I have to see a man about a horse." He winked at me over his shoulder. "How do you feel about mystery stew?"

"With that horse comment, I've suddenly lost my appetite."

It felt wrong leaving the precinct. There was so much we had to follow up on. The hotel had no way of deactivating Juan's keycard remotely, so our killer had the run of the place if he desired. Because of this, two patrol units were permanently stationed outside, and the system was being monitored. If the asshole used the keycard, we'd find out and grab him.

Detective Fennel didn't get anything useful out of Juan's parents, but they gave us access to their son's computer. The cyber unit was in the midst of a deep dive, but we were operating under the assumption Juan Rodriguez just happened to be in the wrong place at the wrong time. Nothing indicated otherwise.

Brad had yet to meet with Mr. Hart or Mr. Stevens, but I knew the names sounded vaguely familiar. They had to be club members. I'd probably seen them a time or two at Spark, which is why Captain Grayson forced me to leave before they showed up. If they didn't volunteer that information, I'd have to check Spark's records. Rick, Kincaid's doorman, kept a running log of who came and went. I could easily ask him when I showed up for my shift tonight. I just needed to come up with a good reason for wanting the information.

As I drove to my cover apartment, thoughts raced through my brain. Becca's words from last night were cryptic and ominous. She warned me to stay away from this. *Don't lie down with dogs.* What the hell did that even mean? She knew who stole the cars, but she was genuinely surprised one of the thieves resorted to murder.

Thieves, plural. Hotel surveillance showed the SUV driver, the killer, and a third man who grabbed the second car. Briefly, I wondered what had become of the other sets of keys they took off Juan's body. Were they even car keys? Four sets. That's what we determined. And, of course, three more vehicles were snatched during the course of the night. At least one of them by a tow truck driver. What the hell was going on? Was any of this even connected?

I let myself into the apartment, more confused now than before I left the station. The crimes seemed random. The vehicles weren't even the same. Two sports cars. Two sedans. And an SUV. *Maybe it's about what's inside the cars.* That's what Becca said, and even that meaningless statement resulted in the killer taking a baseball bat or tire iron to her skull, unless it wasn't the killer but one of the two other men involved in the heist. Regardless, it was the same white SUV, which made them all guilty.

After doing a quick sweep of the apartment to make sure nothing was disturbed, I checked the status of our BOLO. No one had located the vehicle. Patrols were scouring the city for it, but without a plate, it was difficult to find the white SUV in an endless sea of SUVs.

I took a seat in front of my laptop and went through

the notes and photos I'd taken. At one point or another, Axel had several SUVs in his possession. None of them were white. Surveillance photos from the last three months had been taken of people arriving at his club. The only white SUVs were either too large or too small to be the one used in yesterday's crime spree.

"Dammit." I put my hands on my head and circled the apartment, trying to clear my thoughts.

Grabbing the phone, I dialed the captain. "We need to bring in Fox and Emilio. I double-checked their profiles, and neither drives a white SUV. But they saw me with Rebecca Johnson last night. They might know something."

"I heard you the first time you said it, DeMarco," Grayson replied.

"And?" I asked, exasperated.

He let out a huff. "I can authorize officers to bring them in, but they're Axel's guys. They will lawyer up. And they're going to wonder how we got tipped. It'll track straight back to you, and if you aren't compromised yet, you will be. That's a Hail Mary play that I'm not willing to use yet."

"You would if it was Fennel."

"Careful, Detective."

I sucked in a breath. "Get uniforms down to the bar on Amsterdam. It's the dive near Becca's usual corner. She ducks in constantly to use the john or with a john. I'm not sure of the dynamics, but you can show her photo around, ask some questions, and see what shakes loose. I don't care what excuse you come up with, but we can't let this stand."

"Be patient. I'll do my job, and you do yours."

He disconnected, and I resisted the urge to throw the phone into the wall. Instead, I placed it on the table and looked out the window. What were we missing?

I could hear my dad's voice in my head. *Work the scene, Olive. What do you see? What do you hear? What do you smell? What are the commonalities? What are the differences? Forget everything you know. Don't assume anything. Whatever you think is wrong. What is the evidence telling you?*

I checked the time. I had three hours until I was expected at Spark. I couldn't just sit back and twiddle my thumbs for three hours, but I couldn't go traipsing across town to visit the crime scenes either. So I'd have to take a virtual tour. It wasn't that different from our academy training.

Forget everything. The first crime took place yesterday evening in the hotel parking garage, resulting in two stolen vehicles and a dead parking attendant. Ballistics showed the weapon of choice was a forty caliber handgun. There was no DNA, except the valet's. No prints. No hairs. Nothing to indicate anything about our killer's identity. From the security footage, we assumed he was male, average height, athletic build. Nothing stuck out. We were looking for three masked men. One was armed and clearly dangerous.

Emilio, Fox, and Kincaid, I thought and immediately chastised myself for breaking my dad's rules. No assumptions.

And since I couldn't jump to conclusions, I decided to ignore the other three GTAs that occurred in the last twelve hours. Instead, I focused on the obviously linked second crime. The aggravated assault. Again, my mind jumped to the same conclusion, but I pushed it away.

Work the scene. Fact: The killer or one of the crew interacted with Becca prior to the theft and murder, and he knew she talked to me. He left my business card on her body and dumped her at the ER, the same ER where my best friend, Emma, worked, just to make sure I got the message. CSU determined the damage was inflicted by a solid metal object, possibly an aluminum baseball bat, a tire iron, lead pipe, or crowbar. They took photos of the wounds and would narrow the possibilities further, but for now, that's what the preliminary examination indicated.

However, leaving Becca alive posed a huge risk. When she woke up, if she woke up, she could tell us who attacked her. It didn't fit with our killer's profile or his crew's. Whoever killed Juan was careful, but leaving Becca alive was risky. He must be confident Becca wouldn't talk.

I reached for the phone and dialed the rookie officer who responded to the original call. I needed to know two things – where the crime occurred and who Becca feared. It could be her pimp, a john, a boyfriend, her dealer. Anyone. Not only would she have to be afraid of them, but she'd have to depend on them for something. It was the only way they could guarantee her silence.

The rookie promised me he was looking into it, but I hated the thought of some newbie boot screwing this up. It was important. It was a matter of life or death. I couldn't just leave it in the hands of someone still wet behind the ears. Not when lives were on the line.

I grabbed the phone, regretting my decision even as I dialed. "Hey, Dad. I need a favor."

EIGHT

The club wasn't crowded tonight. A few of the regulars drank at the bar, but the dance floor had plenty of space. The back room was closed. No high-stakes poker games or men making exotic wagers. From the gossip around the club, I knew Kincaid had a street race planned in a few days, another epic event guaranteed to attract a ton of attention, so he wanted to keep things quiet. He didn't want more trouble.

After the news broke last night, he knew the police would be knocking on his door any minute, so he took precautions to make sure they wouldn't find anything. He was always careful. That's why I didn't understand why he would beat Becca and leave her in the loading zone outside the emergency room.

My eyes flicked to Fox, who'd been lingering near the VIP area. He was the muscle. He might have done the deed. From what I knew about the man, which wasn't much, he had a history of aggravated assault, assault with a deadly weapon, and attempted murder charges. He also had a short fuse. It was his presence at the bar last night that freaked me out and his constant questions about Becca that sent my radar buzzing. To put it mildly, he had anger issues, but he would have killed her. And I didn't think Kincaid would stop him from eliminating a risk.

I squinted, trying to peer through the shiny silver bars. It was rare that I worked the cage. Being trapped in the box meant Kincaid and his crew could keep an eye on me, and I couldn't do a thing about it. As usual, the club's lighting was a cross between an acid trip and a spaceship. Dancing in a three by three square didn't allow me to question Kincaid or the staff about last night or discover his whereabouts yesterday. The surveillance team said he never left the club, but I knew it was bullshit. He'd ditched them several times before. I didn't believe yesterday was any different.

How much did Axel know? And why did he make himself scarce?

The hairs at the back of my neck prickled. More than likely, he was on to me. Someone said he partied too much the night before and was upstairs in his loft, but I had no way of knowing if it was true. And with the security measures in place, I couldn't exactly go check. For all I knew, Axel was out stealing another car and killing another parking attendant, and I was stuck here with nothing but a hope and a prayer that I'd find some piece of evidence to put the man behind bars. I snorted, realizing the irony of the situation.

The bell sounded for last call. My legs ached, and I was drenched in sweat. Fifteen minutes later, the music quieted and the house lights came on. I looked out at the crowd, no longer blinded by the strobing neons. I'd been at the club for almost eight hours, and I still hadn't spotted the boss.

Normally, the club owner mingled among the throng of guests, catering to them, or running to and from the back room. But tonight, everything was subdued. The high-rollers lounged on the couches while their personal bodyguards and security details stood around looking bored.

Protection details always managed to blend in and stick out at the same time. They all dressed the same, with dark suits and white shirts. It was a sea of drab, punctuated by the ostentatiously rich and their trophy wives, boy toys, and girlfriends. The serious bodyguards didn't wear ties, but even they had the same deadened look on their faces. I couldn't figure out if the really dedicated ones tried to blend in by chatting with the staff and drinking at the bar or if they just didn't give a fuck. But they all had one thing in common; none of them wanted to be here.

The normal crowd didn't bother to show up tonight, as if they knew the modern-day Dionysus was away. But Axel always bid the staff good night, so he had to be here. Somewhere.

The hundred or so club-goers scampered to the door. The dull drone of their conversations, intimate looks, and clandestine touches promised the night wasn't over yet. Vaguely, I wondered how many of the barely legal women had class in the morning. Maybe their sugar daddies would drive them in their fancy sports cars. Damn, this place was the epitome of a mid-life crisis.

Within minutes, only a dozen people remained, mostly Axel's crew. Rick clapped someone on the back as he went out the door, but I didn't get a good look at the departing straggler. Emilio and Fox were at one of the VIP tables in the back, and that's when I spotted our missing god of wine, ecstasy, and probably murder.

Kincaid sat beside them, his back to me, but the dark, styled hair and the tailored jacket could only belong to one person. The three men hunched together over the polished mahogany. I couldn't see what was spread on the table in front of them, but whatever it was kept them occupied.

Emilio caught me watching and waved. *Stupid*, I thought, smiling back, just as Kincaid turned around. His jacket was unbuttoned, and his crisp, white shirt was open at the throat. He said something to the boys, and Fox folded whatever was on the table and tucked it into his pocket. As if that wasn't suspicious.

Kincaid crossed the emptying room and jogged up the steps. He unlocked the cage door and offered his hand. "Liv," he said, his voice deep and sultry, "wonderful performance."

"Thanks." I took his offered hand as he helped me down the steps. I glanced back at the table, but Fox and Emilio were gone.

"Call it a night," Kincaid said, dismissing the bartenders. "We'll finish the clean-up tomorrow." He smiled at Jessica and a few of the other waitresses who were beelining to the locker room and handed me a black silk robe with Spark embroidered in sequins. "You look wrecked. Let me get you something to drink." He went behind the bar.

"Just water," I said, slipping into the robe and fastening it around my waist.

"Sparkling or flat?"

"Flat." I took a step backward, realizing we were alone in the club. "Really, it's not necessary. I have a water bottle in my locker. You don't need to go to any trouble."

"Nonsense." He grabbed a bottle of mineral water and unscrewed the cap before pouring it into a glass. With a jerk of his chin, he dismissed Rick, who went out the front door, locking it behind him. "Are you mad I wouldn't let you come inside to grab your wallet last night?" He brushed past me and placed the glass of water on a table next to one of the sectional sofas. "Fox and Emilio said they ran into you at a bar. You didn't go to Serano's?"

He reached for his phone and scrolled through some details. I heard the muffled conversations of the waitresses heading for the side exit, followed by the sound of the door opening and closing. We were alone.

"No, I didn't. And I'm not mad."

He patted the cushion beside him, and my heart rate kicked up a few notches. Something was up. The bikini top and mini-skirt I wore didn't allow any place to conceal a weapon, except the switchblade which was tucked into a hidden pocket at the small of my back, beneath the thick, rhinestone-studded belt. The academy trained us to take down perps twice our size, but it would be a challenge, particularly in these ridiculous heels.

"Did Fox tell you what happened?" I asked.

Kincaid's gaze flicked to me, and he dropped the phone to the table. "If you have something to confess, now's the time." He leaned back and stared expectantly at me.

"It was stupid, really. Someone left an eight ball as a tip. I don't remember who, but I figured it wouldn't hurt to trade it for cash."

"I see." Kincaid's eyes flicked pointedly to the cushion. The non-verbal order was unmistakable. "I don't allow people to pass drugs around freely."

I crossed the room, stumbling and almost crashing to the ground when my calf suddenly cramped. I winced and hobbled onto the sofa, massaging the knot in my leg.

Kincaid reached down, scooping my legs into his lap and forcing me deeper onto the sofa in a single move. He unbuckled one stiletto heel, letting it drop to the floor before repeating the process with the second one. "Are you dealing inside my club, Liv?"

"No," I said with genuine surprise.

He pressed into the knot in my lower leg. I yelped, but he held tight, keeping me from squirming away. He could do whatever he wanted to me. No one was around to stop him, and even if they were, they all worked for him. He trusted them. With the way he dug his fist into my leg, I knew he didn't trust me.

"Who left them?" he asked again, accentuating the question with a twist of his knuckle.

"I don't know." I thought about implementing various self-defense techniques, but the end result would confirm whatever suspicions were circulating around his brain. He wanted to see how I'd react to the interrogation and the pain.

"Is there anything else I should know about you? Any secrets you haven't shared?"

Just that I'm a few seconds away from knocking your teeth out. My thoughts flashed to the card found in Becca's possession. It didn't list my first name or even first initial, just my rank, last name, and phone number. Even if he suspected I was a cop, he didn't have proof, unless Becca ratted me out. He was testing me, which meant he wasn't certain I was a cop.

"Axel, you're hurting me." I tried to pull away again, but his grip remained firm. "I'm sorry. It won't happen again. I promise." He squeezed my leg harder, and I hissed. Finally, the knot released, and the sharp pain turned into a dull ache.

He relaxed his grip. The pressure eased. "Doesn't that feel better?"

I didn't think he was talking about my leg. "Yes."

"Should something like this happen again, find me. I'll take care of it. You don't need to get hassled by the police. I have enough problems without them poking around. The last thing I need is to have another waitress arrested for possession."

"You're right. It was stupid."

"I'm glad we're in agreement." He leaned back, running his hand gently along my calf. "Who did you pass the drugs to?"

"A hooker who hangs around outside. I've seen a couple of the girls talk to her before, so I figured she was a safe bet." I reached for the water and took a sip.

He slid his hand lower and massaged my ankles, an obvious reward for my cooperation. "You should know, if you continue to affiliate with questionable individuals, I'll have to let you go. The police have a vendetta against me, and after the recent mishap with Wendy, the waitress you replaced, I don't want to give them any more ammunition to fire at me."

"Yes, sir." I tried to pull my legs off his lap, but he held tight. I gave him a cockeyed look. "Seriously, Axel, you have a foot fetish or something?"

"No." He graced me with a wicked smile. All was forgiven. "Just relax." He dug his thumb into the ball of my foot, and my head fell back. Killer or not, he had skilled hands, capable of inflicting pain or pleasure. "According to the log, you missed your last two breaks. These heels must be hell. I can't just let you hobble around, particularly this late at night."

"I won't hobble," I insisted. "My bike's outside."

"Still, I should have made sure someone let you out of the cage. I didn't realize the staff needed my constant supervision."

"Where were you?"

"Upstairs."

"You must have thrown quite the rager last night. Or was it a family emergency, like Fox said?"

He looked confused, and I wondered if he forgot the lie he told me. "It wasn't much of a party. It was a meeting with my investors. Boring business stuff." He turned to face me, hitting me with the full force of his rugged good looks. Yet, another man who thought he could charm me. I was getting tired of this routine. "Your night was probably a lot more exciting."

"Selling coke and getting felt up by Emilio. Real exciting. Damn, I could be the inspiration for a comedy movie or a murder mystery." I stared at him, gauging his reaction.

Axel's face dropped, and his eyes darkened. "I'll take care of it."

"I didn't say—"

"I'll take care of it." Leaving no room for protest, he slid off the couch and poured the rest of the bottle of water into my glass. "Let me make a call."

My phone was in my locker. I couldn't exactly send a message to the boys outside. What the hell was Axel about to do? Regardless, we had eyes on him. And an eyewitness – me. If something happened to Emilio, he wouldn't be able to deny it. Maybe this was for the best.

Axel hit a button and went into the back room, closing the door. I couldn't hear his words, and I didn't dare move closer. Finally, he returned to the main room, tucked the phone away, and went behind the bar to pour himself a drink. "Are you sure I can't interest you in anything harder?" His lip twitched slightly.

"I should get going. Thanks for the foot rub." I picked up my glass and returned it to the kitchen and grabbed my shoes. I was halfway to the locker room when I heard the pounding at the front door and the announcement.

NINE

"Police. Open up."

Axel snorted and looked straight at me. "See what I mean?" He disengaged the security system and opened the door. "Gentlemen, we're closed. If you were hoping for a drink, you'll have to come back another night."

"Cut the crap." Detective Fennel looked past Kincaid and into the club. "I have a few questions about some of your members. May I come in?"

Kincaid stepped back, allowing the police to enter. Fennel pushed his way inside and glanced around, spotting me frozen between the bar and rear hallway. "Anyone else here?"

"I don't believe so." Kincaid sauntered back to the bar and picked up his drink. He took a sip and rested his elbow against the shiny surface. His eyes remained on my partner.

"Who the hell is she?" Fennel asked, jerking his chin at me. He scoffed at the silk robe. "Did we interrupt something?"

"Mind telling me why you're here, Detective?" Kincaid asked, his voice adopting an edge.

"Do you know an Eric Hart or Lawrence Stevens?" Fennel asked.

"You know I do." Kincaid glanced at me. "Go get changed and go home, Liv."

"Ma'am, stay right there," one of the uniforms said.

"Oh for fuck's sake." Kincaid rubbed his eyes. "It's late. I'm in no mood for games. Just tell me what this is about. And leave my waitress out of it."

"Waitress, huh? That wouldn't have been my first guess." Fennel made a show of looking at his notepad. "Have you seen the news lately, Mr. Kincaid? You wouldn't happen to know anything about the stolen sports cars, would you?"

"No."

"Your juvie record says otherwise."

"Those records are sealed," Kincaid hissed. "I'm a legitimate businessman. And your accusation sounds like slander."

"I apologize," Fennel said sarcastically. "Since Mr. Hart and Mr. Stevens are members of your club, I was just wondering if you noticed anyone paying attention to them or their vehicles. Perhaps there was an altercation or a disagreement, or someone expressed an interest in the cars?"

"Not that I recall."

"It's a private club. Members only." Fennel looked up from his notepad and surveyed the room, which looked a lot different with the lights on. "We could really use a list of names."

"Not without a court order. My client list is confidential."

"What kinds of things go on here?"

Axel let out a growl. "I doubt you'll ever find out. Civil servants can't afford my membership fees."

Fennel pointed the end of his pen at me. "You said she's a waitress. What's your name, ma'am?"

"Liv," I swallowed, "Olivia Bell."

"Have you ever served Mr. Hart or Mr. Stevens?"

"I don't know the guests by name," I said.

"Leave her alone." Axel's reaction seemed genuine, and I hoped that meant my cover remained intact.

"Maybe this will help." Fennel reached into his pocket and removed photos of Hart, Stevens, and their stolen cars. "Recognize them or their rides?" He made a show of looking me up and down. "Maybe you let one of them take you for a ride."

"That is enough," Axel said.

"Then why is she dressed like that?" Fennel asked.

"We were short-staffed, so Liv was gracious enough to fill in for one of the dancers." Axel finished his drink and put it down on the bar. He crossed to the cage. "She dances in here. Fully clothed. Do you want to check my permits or security footage?"

"It wouldn't hurt." Fennel nodded to one of the uniforms to get on that.

"Then get a warrant. I run a tight ship, Detective. It's a shame something happened to Mr. Hart and Mr. Stevens' cars, but it didn't happen here. So what do you really want to ask me?"

Fennel licked his lips. "Just following up on a lead, and you're the common denominator." Fennel flipped to another page. "Would you mind telling me where you were yesterday around seven?"

Axel poured another drink, holding the bottle toward Brad. "Oh, right. You're on duty."

"Sir, please answer the question."

I stared at my partner, seeing his gaze shift to the bottle for a millisecond. Hopefully, Axel didn't notice. I was probably the only one who would.

"I was here," Kincaid insisted.

"What about between the hours of midnight and four a.m.?" Brad wheedled.

"Still here." Axel forced a calm friendliness into his voice.

"Do you know this woman?" Fennel handed him a photo of Rebecca Johnson. Axel glanced at it but didn't react. "What about you?" Brad turned the photo in my direction.

"Um..." I sputtered, wondering what my partner hoped to gain by questioning me.

But as usual, Brad knew precisely what he was doing. My flustered response caused Axel to intervene.

"Let me see that again." Kincaid took the photo from Fennel and studied it. His expression was unreadable. He might as well have been reading the classifieds. "I don't know her. Maybe I've seen her, but I can't say for certain. She looks like trouble, and as a rule, I avoid trouble."

"Of course, you do." Fennel looked around the empty club. "You mind if I look around?"

"I do."

"I thought you said you didn't have anything to hide."

"I don't, but it's late. Now please leave."

"We're not through yet," Brad said.

Axel picked up his phone. "In that case, I'm calling my attorney."

"You're well within your right to contact counsel, Mr. Kincaid, but if you do that, I'll have to make this official. Is that what you want? Right now, we're just two guys having a conversation. As soon as you account for your whereabouts yesterday and provide someone who can verify them, I'll get out of your hair."

"I was here all night. I even slept upstairs."

"Can anyone vouch for you?" Fennel asked.

"My investors." Kincaid chuckled and toasted in my direction. "And Liv."

"You were here last night, ma'am?" Brad asked.

"Briefly," I said, wondering if Kincaid expected me to lie for him. Was this another test? "I stopped by around nine or ten." I looked to Axel for verification, and he nodded. "I left my wallet here. So I called Axel's office. He said there was a private event."

"A business meeting. I can get you names," Kincaid offered.

"Did you actually see Mr. Kincaid?" Brad asked, even though he knew the truth. But we were doing our best to role-play.

"No, she didn't," Axel said before I could answer.

"Take down her information in case we have any other questions, and I will take that list of names." Fennel handed Kincaid a sheet of paper and a pen.

"On second thought, bite me."

"You really want to do it the hard way?" Fennel asked.

Axel snickered. "Do you?"

"Ma'am," one of the officers said, holding out his pen, "your information."

I eyed Axel, as if asking permission, and he nodded. I wrote down my cover details, wondering if the uniform was aware of the ruse or if Fennel kept him in the dark.

Fennel eyed me again. "Put on some clothes and get out of here."

"Finally," I muttered, exasperated.

I went to the locker room and changed into my clothes and put my leather jacket on. When I returned to the main room, Kincaid wore a matching set of bracelets. My partner must have found something because arresting Kincaid prematurely would not work in our favor.

"Axel?" I asked, making sure I kept my eyes focused on him.

"It's okay, Liv. Be careful going home. The crazies are out, and clearly, we can't depend on the cops to keep people safe."

"Go on, ma'am," one of the uniforms said, opening the door to the club.

As I climbed onto my bike, I turned and caught one last glimpse of the men as Kincaid was loaded into the back of a squad car.

TEN

After Kincaid was carted off, I returned to the apartment, the status of my cover precarious. I wanted to go to the station, but Kincaid was there. Soon, his lawyer would be and possibly his crew. I sent a message to dispatch and had a patrol sit on Emilio in case Kincaid's threat turned into more than a few stern words. At least with the arrest, it wouldn't seem abnormal to have patrols monitoring his crew.

Then I sent a text to my partner. *What the hell did you dig up?*

A moment later, my phone rang. I looked at the ID and hit answer. "Well?" I asked.

"Axel Kincaid left the hotel an hour before Juan Rodriguez was killed," Brad said. "He wasn't a guest. In fact, we have no idea why he was even there. We spotted him in the lobby when we were reviewing the interior footage."

"What was he doing there?"

"Nothing."

"Nothing?"

"He read a magazine and used the john."

"There aren't any cameras in the bathroom," I said.

"Yeah, I know. I checked it out, but we didn't find anything."

"Are you sure?"

"Feel free to look again."

I laughed. Brad always got cranky when he was tired. And since it was after three in the morning, he was probably exhausted. "Maybe I will." I blew out a breath. "You should know, there's a chance Kincaid might be on to me."

"Did he hurt you? What did he say, Liv?"

"It was weird. We'll talk about it later."

"Liv," Brad wheedled, "you sure you're okay? I don't know what I walked in on tonight, but it didn't look good."

"I'm fine. Let's put this thing to bed."

"It looks like that's what Kincaid planned to do with you."

I rolled my eyes. "Good night, Brad. Call if there are any developments."

"You do the same."

A backup team remained on standby two minutes out, just in case I really was blown and Kincaid was as good an actor as Fennel and me. It was almost five a.m. before I settled down enough to sleep. Working nights in a club and days at the precinct made sleep nearly impossible. But this should be over soon. Kincaid was in custody. We placed him at the hotel around the time of the thefts. We had our killer or one of the killer's accomplices. Once we convinced Axel to roll on his crew, we'd get warrants for everything and find out what was really going on in the back room of that club.

You know it's not that simple, the voice in my head muttered. I rolled over and stared at the neon green glow of the clock, unable to sleep. Emma was working graveyard at the hospital. She wouldn't mind an early morning call, so I dialed and waited.

"Hey, what are you doing up so early?" Emma asked.

"Waiting for some things to shake loose on a late night bust. How's Becca?"

"No change."

"How are you?" I asked.

Emma snickered. "I can't complain. Well, I could, but if I do, I'll just sound like an ungrateful bitch. So anyway, moving on, Maria called the other day."

"My mom?"

"Yep."

"What did she want?"

"She wanted to know if I was coming to family dinner."

"I'm sorry. I forgot to ask you."

"Sure, sure. It's just because you're jealous your mom likes me more than you."

I laughed. "Well, she does. You're the daughter she always wanted."

"Liv," Emma said patiently, "you know that's not true."

"No. It is, but it's okay." The awkward silence filled the air. "You can't leave me in suspense. Are you coming to dinner?"

"That depends. Are you going to be there?"

"I'm working on it."

"Well, work faster. She wants my answer by Friday. And I don't want to go to another one of your family functions if you aren't going to be there. It's always so awkward. Your dad never knows what to say to me, and your mom gives me the third degree on who I'm dating and when I'm going to settle down and get married. Do you remember the time she tried to fix me up with your cousin?"

"I'm so glad she likes you more than me."

"Shit," Em said, "someone's coding. I gotta go." She hung up before I could say another word.

I stared at the end call message. Was this really my life? Or was my life just another fake identity? I'd been working undercover assignments for nearly two years. I didn't even have my own apartment anymore because I was rarely me. In between assignments, I'd crash at Emma's or my parents'. At times, I felt like I was losing myself. Right now was one of those moments. I needed to get some sleep. I'd feel better once I was back at my desk in the precinct.

The sun came up before I managed to fall asleep. And when I finally did, there was a knock on the door. Brad. It had to be. I brushed my hair back and peered through the peephole.

Holy shit. I checked the apartment. Nothing linking to the police investigation or my identity was in sight. My badge and gun were locked away, along with any files I had brought along to peruse. Units were outside. I palmed my cell phone, tucking it into the pocket of my robe, ready to send an SOS.

Reluctantly, I slid the chain off the door and turned the lock. "What are you doing here?" I asked. "How do you know where I live?"

"Your job application," Axel replied. He didn't wait for an invitation before entering my apartment. "I just wanted to make sure you were okay. I didn't know if the police brought you in for questioning."

"No."

"Good." He paused, struggling to come up with something to say. It was odd for a man who always seemed completely in charge. "Thanks for helping me out back there."

"I just told the truth."

"I'm glad you did. Lies lead to more trouble."

"They released you?"

He took a seat on the couch and rubbed his eyes. "Spark caters to a certain crowd. People who live large tend to frequent my club and also tend to be the same people in power. I just needed to make a few calls." He snorted. "The police don't have anything to hold me on. I haven't done anything wrong. I'm not a thug. I don't steal cars or kill people."

"The police seem to think so."

"What do you think, Liv? Do you think I'm a monster?"

"No." I shrugged the question away.

He sighed. "I don't know what you've heard about me, but I have a past. I understand why I'd be their prime suspect. But they have no proof, and until they do, they need to back off."

It sounded like a warning, and again, I wondered if I was compromised.

His cold eyes stared at me. "I need you tomorrow night."

"Okay." I gave him a confused look. "I don't think I'm scheduled to work, but I can come in."

"Not work. I'll pick you up around midnight. Dress comfortably, but not that comfortably." He eyed the ratty t-shirt and pajama shorts beneath my robe. "Now get some sleep. You can have tonight off. I imagine the police will be back in force, and I don't want to give them easy access to you. You've already done enough."

Again, his words resonated as a threat. I didn't react. Instead, I remained on the couch, watching as he let himself out of the apartment.

He was planning something. Unfortunately, I had no idea what it was, but it involved me.

ELEVEN

He remained outside her apartment. She was smooth. The lies she told rolled off her tongue easily. She had a reasonable explanation for everything. How much longer could she carry on the charade before she was caught? How much longer could he wait?

A glance at her bedroom window ensured she was asleep, so he stepped out of the non-descript minivan. In running gear and a hoodie, the surveillance unit wouldn't recognize him. After all, they didn't even notice when he parked the van two spaces behind them. They weren't looking for a van. He wasn't even sure if they would notice a flashy muscle car. They were focused on her, just like he was.

He jogged down the street, his soles slapping against the pavement. Aside from a few people walking their dogs, it was too early for most people to be out. He jogged past her motorcycle, the racing bike glistening in the morning mist.

She only rode it to the club. It was part of her cover, and he had no interest in her lies. Liv DeMarco interested him, not Olivia Bell. And that meant the detective's car might come in handy, especially since she believed no one knew about it. It's why she kept it on a side street.

He continued jogging along the sidewalk, running in place while he looked both ways before crossing. He circled around, so the van wouldn't see him turn down the same side street. It was probably unnecessary to take such precautions, but he wanted to be careful.

Since the police came knocking at Spark's door, they obviously didn't heed his first warning, but he'd make them listen this time. He gave her the chance to back off, but she didn't comply. She left him no choice. He slowed several feet from her car, putting his hands on top of his head as if trying to catch his breath. Then he knelt down, pretending to tie his shoe as he examined the undercarriage and removed the device from his pocket. It would all be over soon.

*   *   *

Captain Grayson left a message, warning me to stay out of sight. So I didn't go to the precinct. Instead, I swung by the hospital to check on Becca before heading to the hotel. Her condition remained unchanged, but CSU found skin beneath her fingernails. They were testing it to see if it was a match to anyone in the system, but DNA took time. Typically 24-72 hours. We had at least another day to go before we'd get the results.

When I called Brad, his phone went straight to voicemail. That wasn't a good sign. Hopefully, he was asleep. Maybe his battery was dead. I checked the time. If I didn't hear from him in the next four hours, I'd go to his apartment. In the meantime, I had plenty to keep me busy.

"It looks like you're having fun," Laura Mackenzie said, entering the hotel room. "How did you convince the department to swing for a room? And can we get spa treatments and room service while we're here?"

"I wish." I rubbed the kink in my neck.

"Everything okay?" she asked, opening her computer bag and taking out her laptop and peripherals. "Where's Fennel? Shouldn't he be assisting you?"

"He's not my assistant. He's my partner."

"Is there a difference?" She cracked a wicked smile and went to work. Mac was the resident computer expert at the precinct, at least as far as I was concerned. She was young with no formal education. At the age of sixteen, she was arrested for hacking the Pentagon. She finished high school while in federal custody and worked for the Feds in exchange for not being sentenced to hard time. After serving her time with them, the police department hired her on the commissioner's insistence, but most of the guys were intimidated by the spunky hacker turned hero and steered clear, which worked great for me.

"Not really, but don't tell Fennel." I winked, sliding her a disk. "See if there's anything worthwhile here. And if there's time, do you think you might be able to get an ID on the driver? Or the tow truck's VIN? Cyber division said it wasn't possible, but I thought you might have a few tricks up your sleeve."

She cracked her knuckles. "No problem." While Mac ran the hotel guests through facial recognition and enhanced the images of the tow truck driver in question, I told her about the investigation.

"I think there's a tattoo under the guy's sleeve, but I can't make it out. Do you think you can work some magic?" I asked.

"Magic's my middle name, but this might take a

while," she warned. "Maybe an hour or two."

"I've got time, if you're game. The room's ours for as long as we need it."

"Why, Detective DeMarco, I didn't realize you had other plans in mind," Mac teased, "but I'm game. Go find us a couple of studs. I'll crack open the mini-bar, order some pay-per-view, and get ready to party."

I rolled my eyes in order to hide my smile. "I need to check the men's room."

"I guess that's one way to see what they're packing without having to wait 'til the end of the night."

Ignoring her, I left the room and returned to the lobby. A patrol unit remained near the front entrance. Another one was positioned in the parking garage. Crime scene tape roped off the section where the murder occurred, but aside from that, it was just business as usual inside the hotel. Life went on, just not for Juan Rodriguez.

The men's room was right off the lobby, and I knocked politely on the door. "Housekeeping," I called, pushing it open a crack. "Anyone in here?"

"Just a sec," a guy replied. I waited in the doorway for him to leave. "All yours."

"Did you wash your hands?"

He squinted, taking too long to think about something that should have been a simple yes. From his furrowed brow, one would think he was working out a geometry proof. "Uh..."

"No, you didn't." I pushed the door open. "Last chance."

He returned to the bathroom and stood in front of the automatic sink. I handed him a paper towel, eyeing the three stalls. He dried his hands and handed me five bucks.

"Have a nice day," he said.

Well, if the cop thing didn't work out, I could

probably make a living as a bathroom attendant. I waited for the door to swing closed before flipping the lock. The three stalls were empty, and I gave the four urinals against the wall a cursory look. Fennel was right; there was nothing here.

But I was stubborn, so I examined the fixtures, finding nothing above or below any of the sinks or urinals. I opened the soap dispensers and paper towel dispensers, but nothing was hiding inside. Next, I stepped into the first stall, checked inside the toilet paper dispenser, behind the door, and in the toilet tank.

"What the hell are you doing, Liv?" I asked myself. Fennel would have done this. I stepped out of the stall. Without any windows or other exits, it was unlikely Kincaid could have used this as a dead drop. The only other possibility was he met someone inside.

Mac was already working that angle, so there wasn't much left for me to do. My outing to the hotel was quickly turning into a bust. On a whim, I checked for disturbed or cracked tiles, but I didn't find any hidey-holes.

While I was washing my hands, the light above the third stall flickered. I watched it in the mirror. The wiring hung down from the end of the light, and I turned to examine one of the other fluorescents. The wiring on the others was taut, disappearing into a small hole drilled in the ceiling tile.

I entered the third stall and looked up. Ceiling tiles made great places to stash contraband, so carefully, I hoisted myself onto the toilet seat, balancing on the edges. I pushed the ceiling tile up, ducking my face away as dust rained down on me. After moving the tile out of the way, I flicked on my flashlight and peered inside.

"You're never going to hear the end of this, Fennel."

Triumphant, I slipped on a pair of gloves and retrieved the zippered baggie from its hiding spot. Inside was a hotel keycard and a stack of cash. I leafed through the money. Five grand.

I tucked the money back into the bag and removed the keycard. It was black, just like the card stolen from Juan Rodriguez. But Kincaid was in the bathroom before Rodriguez was killed and before his keycard was stolen. So how did this card get here? And who did it belong to?

After calling it in, I had one of the patrolmen sit with the evidence. I tapped my nails impatiently against my thigh. I wanted to ask the hotel manager about the keycard. Maybe it belonged to a guest. Maybe a second one had gone missing. Either way, I wanted to know where it came from and what it unlocked, but we needed to dust it for prints first. Contaminating newly discovered evidence would not be helpful.

Thirty minutes later, the van pulled up. Techs came inside. They dusted the card, finding it wiped clean. As soon as they were done with it, I took it to the front desk while they examined the ceiling inside the restroom, the baggie, and the cash.

The hotel manager said the keycard belonged to one of the maids, and it had been reported missing two days ago. That was the same day Rodriguez was killed and the cars were stolen. I let out an annoyed huff. The hotel manager should have mentioned this sooner, when the crime occurred. The keycard allowed access to all the guestrooms.

Maybe Kincaid asked someone to swipe the card. When he was finished, he left it in the ceiling tile, along with payment. I frowned, uncertain of my theory. Something was going on inside this hotel. I just didn't know what.

"Did you find anything?" I asked, returning to the restroom.

"Traces of cocaine." The tech held up the swab, the bright purple tip confirming his statement.

"What about prints?" I asked.

"We found several partials, but the scanner is having trouble spitting out an ID. We'll need to run them through the computer at the lab."

"Okay. Get on that, and let me know what you find." I looked at the patrolman. "Until further notice, we need the bathroom roped off. No one in or out, especially hotel staff."

"Yes, ma'am."

"I'll be down the hall if you need me." On my way back to the room, I tried Brad again. This time it didn't go straight to voicemail, so at least he turned his phone back on. However, he still didn't answer. "Dammit." I sent a text with instructions to meet at the hotel and checked the time. Two hours. If I didn't hear from him in two hours, I'd send a search party. Or I could probably get Mac to ping his phone.

"Hey, I have another assignment for you," I said, stepping inside. "Possibly two."

While Mac worked on the computer, I made a few calls to the insurance companies to find out if they had any insight to offer regarding the stolen vehicles or their owners. They didn't, and after checking the crime databases for anything related to Towers Wrecker Service and examining the business profile, I was still no closer to figuring out who purchased the tow truck. According to DMV records, the truck wasn't registered to anyone. It, along with the rest of the wrecking service assets, had been sent to a scrapyard. I wrote down the address, figuring it was another long shot. After all, the company went out of business five years ago.

Why target these specific individuals? The hotel garage had been filled with exotic cars during the event, so why would the thieves steal three less valuable vehicles later that same night? If they wanted a bigger score, they shouldn't have killed Juan. They should have driven off with the two sports cars and came back and grabbed two more. I thought back to my original theory. We weren't dealing with the same crew. Kincaid might be the hottest game in town with his penchant for exotic racing cars, even if we couldn't prove it, but someone else performed the other jobs. Axel wouldn't waste his time on two sedans and an SUV, unless they were tricked out in gold.

I closed my eyes. Becca said it was about what was inside the cars. Which cars did she mean? At the time, I thought she meant the two exotic rides, but maybe she meant the other three thefts. I didn't know about those when I confronted her, but she might have known they were going to get stolen. Or there had been others. Or I was losing my mind.

What if our assumptions were wrong? Maybe we were looking at two separate cases. We needed to separate the facts, starting with our newest evidence.

I dialed the officer in charge of Becca's case, and he passed me off to Wes Harding, a vice detective. I swallowed. Since Becca was a pro, it made sense for vice to be involved, but I knew the only reason Detective Harding caught her case was because my dad made a call.

"Any leads?" I asked.

Harding cleared his throat. "We believe we found where she was attacked. We found blood inside an abandoned warehouse near Becca's normal stomping grounds."

"Any witnesses?"

"Maybe. A few of the other girls who work that

territory might have seen something, but if it was their pimp, they'll be too afraid to talk."

I thought for a second, but I didn't have any other contacts in the area besides Becca. Becca was the common denominator. She could give us answers.

"Anything else?" I asked.

"Yeah," Harding said, "we found the murder weapon. A crowbar. We didn't find any prints, so we have no way of tracing it back to the killer. I put feelers out. We're checking nearby security cameras, but it doesn't look promising."

My insides clenched. "Rebecca's dead?"

"She succumbed to her injuries two hours ago."

TWELVE

"You all right?" Fennel asked. "If you need to cry or something, I'll get you a tissue."

"Where the hell have you been?"

Brad looked away. "Busy, but I brought you coffee. Figured you could use it after last night. Hell, we could both use it." Fennel handed me one of the two cups in his hand, which I put down. When he put his beside mine, I picked up his cup and took a sip. At least he wasn't drinking on the job. Based on the amount of aftershave he slathered on, I knew where he'd been when I called.

"Where's mine?" Mac asked.

"Sorry. Liv didn't tell me it was a party."

"Yeah, I'm still waiting on the studs to arrive." She shot a look at Fennel. "Unless we're supposed to share."

He gave me a quizzical look. "So what did you find in the bathroom that was so important it couldn't wait?"

"Come on. I'll show you." I led him out of the hotel room and pushed him into an alcove next to the ice machine. "Are you still drunk?"

"No, just hungover."

"What happened to being around if I needed you? Didn't you say you were going to stop by my apartment? Because Kincaid sure did."

"Shit." Fennel slammed the side of his fist into the ice machine, causing several cubes to drop. He squeezed the bridge of his nose, the headache obvious. "He's taunting us. He's playing with us. That sicko is enjoying it. What did he want?"

"I don't know. He wants me to go somewhere with him tomorrow night, and he wants me to stay away from Spark until then." I sighed. "Becca's dead."

"I know." He stared right at me but saw something from a long time ago. "We said no more bodies. That we wouldn't let anyone else get killed."

"Brad?"

He shook away the thought and blinked. "What did you find in the bathroom?"

"A bag with money and a hotel keycard hidden in the ceiling. They found traces of cocaine, but I don't know if it's related."

"Typical dead drop. Someone leaves the cash, and someone else picks it up and delivers the drugs. Or vice versa. Given the keycard, I'd say maybe something was getting delivered to the room."

"More drugs?"

Brad shrugged. "Perhaps, or something too large or too heavy to stash in the ceiling."

I thought for a moment. "There's something going on inside this hotel, and since two staff keycards have gone missing, someone who works here could be involved."

"I'll take another look at Juan Rodriguez. He looked clean, but appearances can be deceiving." Brad stepped away from the ice machine and glanced down the hallway. "The hotel manager's been cooperating, so see if he'll give us access to their footage for the last couple of weeks. If not, call your boyfriend and see if he can get us a warrant. Based on what you found in the ceiling, it shouldn't be much of a stretch."

"Winters is not my boyfriend," I hissed.

Brad smirked, the first reassuring sign that he hadn't fallen too deeply down the rabbit hole. "And yet, you knew exactly who I was talking about. Care to explain that one, DeMarco?"

"Screw you."

"Did you make Winters the same offer because that would explain why he's so smitten?"

I slapped his arm, a smile tugging at my lips. We had to be more than the job. Or it would eat us alive.

"All right." Fennel scrubbed his hands down his face. "You stay here, and see what you can dig up. Try to stay out of sight. Kincaid's under surveillance, but we don't want any of his buddies to spot you either. For all we know, someone in the hotel could be working with him."

"I doubt it."

"Why?"

"He wouldn't have needed to hide the keycard in the ceiling tile." A terrible thought went through my mind. What if the items in the ceiling have nothing to do with Kincaid? "I think we're looking at two crews. The three vehicles and the tow truck driver don't fit the bill for the three-man team who performed the heist here and killed Rodriguez."

"Yeah, but you saw Fox's text. Five cars."

"Maybe that was something else."

"Maybe we need to stop speculating and figure this thing out." He gave me an odd look. "What possessed you to look in the ceiling?"

"I saw it in a movie."

Fennel snorted. "Wow."

"Plus, I couldn't let you be right."

"That's more like it." He started to leave, but I stopped him.

"Check Rodriguez's car. Becca told me it wasn't about the rides but what's inside them. And stay away from the bottle."

"Yes, ma'am." Fennel saluted with two fingers and disappeared down the corridor.

I returned to the lobby and spoke to the hotel manager again. Hotel security escorted me to their office, where I clicked through the footage and asked them to save the requested files onto a separate drive. With the USB in hand, I returned to our suite. Poor Mac, she had her hands full.

"Here," I said, offering her my untouched coffee. It was the least I could do.

"Thanks."

With Becca's death hanging over my head, I was on a mission. Whoever did this would pay. The bastard was a coward. He wanted to get to me, but he did it by going after her. Clearly, he didn't have the balls to go toe-to-toe with the police department, but I wasn't going to give him a choice.

Mac printed a photo enhancement from the hotel security feed. "Him," she said.

"You're sure?"

"It's the same guy." She pulled up the image of the tow truck driver. We didn't get a clear look at his face in either photo, but the small portion of his tattoo visible beneath his shirt sleeve was identical. The tow truck driver who stole the SUV later that night had been inside the hotel an hour before Kincaid entered the bathroom.

"Track his movements," I said. "We need to know where he went inside the hotel, who he spoke to, and if he stepped foot inside the lobby bathroom."

I examined his face. He wore a cap and sunglasses to conceal his features. His shoes looked like run-of-the-mill work boots, and he wore a plain white short-sleeve polo with jeans. Probably ninety percent of the men in the city owned the same outfit, but we might be able to ID him from his ink.

Taking a photo of the image, I texted Detective Harding. Maybe one of Becca's associates would recognize the tattoo. After he promised to ask around, I put the phone down. What I needed more than anything was for the lab to get back to me on the prints found on the bag and the money.

The tattooed tow truck driver had to link to Kincaid. It was the only reason both men would have been inside the hotel. According to Mac, they both visited the same men's room, roughly an hour apart. The stolen and seemingly unrelated SUV had to link to the two high-end thefts. It was all connected. I just didn't know how or why.

"According to the hotel feed, our tattooed suspect hung around inside the bar and made a few calls on his cell phone before ducking into the men's room."

"How did he pay for his drinks?" I asked.

"Cash," she said. "You're not going to get an ID that way." She watched the footage again. "He doesn't have a room key, so I doubt he's a guest. And he left right after he visited the men's room. He simply walked away. The exterior cameras lose sight of him pretty quickly."

"That would have given him plenty of time to change clothes, rendezvous with the SUV, and steal a car and kill a man." Running through my options, I decided on my next course of action. "The prison database keeps a record of tattoos."

"So does the military," Mac said.

"Yeah, well, I'll start with the prison system and go from there." With just a partial, it would be difficult to search for a match since I didn't know what the sweeping dark curves might represent. It could be some sort of tribal pattern, the tail of a dragon, or anything in between. At least we knew the location on his body. Really, how many men could have tattoos on their right bicep?

The number of search results nearly floored me. *It's not a prison tatt*, I reminded myself. The artwork was too elaborate for rudimentary tools to have made. I spent hours clicking through the pages while Mac continued working on everything else, but in the end, I didn't find the driver's tattoo. We still didn't have an ID.

"Think, Liv. Think," I muttered.

Mac snorted. "Does that help?"

"Sometimes." A pounding headache was forming behind my eyes. On a whim, I tried a reverse image search on the partial. It didn't come up with an exact match, but it did lead to several websites. Tattoo artists liked to keep portfolios of their work, and a few had similar styles. One of them might have inked the guy. Now I just had to put in the legwork. "I'm going to follow up and see what I can find. Are you good here?"

"Yep, just waiting on the strippers and room service to arrive." She winked at me. "Good luck, Detective."

THIRTEEN

The red dot on the screen turned left. Maybe she missed her turn. He waited, but she didn't correct or take the next exit. She wasn't going to the precinct or returning to the apartment. Where was she headed?

An uneasiness filled him. The red dot turned again. He broke out in a cold sweat.

"No. No. No." He stared in horror. It couldn't be. How was she tracking him? How did she know about the studio? He was careful. Frantically, he thought about the hotel. No one was left to squeal. Unless...no. It wasn't possible.

He reached for the remote trigger, the silver of the handgun catching his eye. That had to go. She was on to him, which meant her partner might be too. Or any of those other twats at the police station. Arrogance would be the final nail in his coffin. He had to correct his mistake. He couldn't let this continue another second. How could he have been so stupid?

He flipped the switch, letting out a breath when the red dot vanished from the screen. Now to cover his tracks.

*　　*　　*

Rush hour traffic was a bitch. I turned down another street, glad to be picking up speed. The tattoo parlor was just a few blocks away. I cut into the other lane, and that's when I heard a metallic pop. My rear tires jumped, and I checked the mirror. What the hell was that? My eyes went to the dashboard. Could it be a flat? None of the lights were on. The car was dead.

Before I could do anything, the subcompact, that had been riding my ass, slammed into my bumper. After that, everything happened in the blink of an eye. I tried to correct, but the steering wheel seized. The driver behind me must have attempted to avoid the collision by pulling to the right, which forced the nose of my car across the double yellow line and into oncoming traffic.

Horns blared, and a pickup clipped my front fender. The force and speed of the hit whipped my car around. More horns. Screeching brakes. I looked to the side just in time to see a city bus t-bone the passenger door. The inside crushed forward. Any second, I'd be crushed too.

The bus driver practically stood on the brakes, doing his best to hold the bus steady as it pushed my car sideways down the median until I crashed into the cement divider. The metal shrieked, crumbling under the pressure. Thankfully, the bus came to a stop, leaving me wedged between it and the cement divider.

I reached for my phone, but it was dead, just like my car. I took a breath, assessing the situation. At least three cars were stopped on both sides of the road. Traffic had slowed to a crawl and continued to move past in the outside lanes. My windows were shattered. But by some miracle, I was mostly unscathed.

"Are you okay?" the bus driver asked. He had gotten out and was standing beside my pinned vehicle. "I called 911. They're on the way."

I unhooked my seatbelt and turned to check my door. It wouldn't budge. The rear door smashed inward, along with most of the frame. A foot closer, and that would have been me. I felt a little woozy, probably from the realization that I'd been extremely lucky rather than from any actual trauma.

"I'm fine." I shifted in my seat as I collected a few scattered items from the floor.

"Try not to move." The bus driver turned back to his bus. "Shit." He looked at the damage and his frightened and annoyed passengers. "I'll be right back." He returned to the bus, and I saw him speaking into his radio.

Before he returned to check on me again, the fire department arrived with a few ambulances in tow. I badged them before they could slip the c-collar around my neck and waited for them to pop out my cracked windshield. I let them follow protocol to get me out of the car. Figuring since I already ruined one civil servant's day, I didn't need to ruin more.

"What the hell happened?" one of them asked.

"I don't know. My car just stopped."

A second truck arrived from the other direction, and they blocked off the affected lanes. I took the collar off my neck and dismissed the paramedics, ushering them away to check on the other drivers and the people on the bus. I looked at the crushed tin can.

"You were lucky," one of the firefighters said.

A patrol car pulled up, and I gave my statement and submitted to a breathalyzer. Thank heavens Brad didn't spike his coffee, or I would have had to explain that. I sat in the front seat of the squad car while I watched tow trucks arrive to pick up the subcompact which initially hit me. The pickup never stopped. It fled the scene, so the police issued a BOLO.

"That's the last time I ever take a car from the motor pool," I said.

The officer chuckled. "Yeah, well, it's not like they give us much of a choice."

After most of the scene had been cleared, firefighters swept glass and debris out of the street and shoveled it into my car. Something metallic caught my eye, and I peered into what was left of the back seat to see what it was. It looked like a piece of the fender, but it had circuits and computer chips attached.

What the hell is that? I reached for my phone again, remembering it was dead. Great. The one time I needed it to work. Before I left the hotel, it was fully charged. Maybe it had been damaged in the crash.

"Can I borrow your radio?" I asked the officer.

A few minutes later, Fennel pulled to a stop behind the patrol car. "Liv," he ran to me, "are you okay?" He assessed my appearance. "You ought to get checked out." He ran a flashlight in front of my eyes and poked at a scratch near my eyebrow. "Does your head hurt?"

I slapped the flashlight away. "Not any more than it did before the accident."

He frowned at my answer. His gaze went to the remnants of the car as it was loaded onto a tow truck. "How the hell are you still alive?"

"She must have a guardian angel," one of the firefighters said.

"Was anyone hurt?" Fennel asked.

"Just a few bumps and bruises," the firefighter replied. "Nothing serious."

"Mostly a lot of annoyed drivers," the patrolman

added.

With everything squared away, I climbed into the passenger seat of Brad's car, wincing at a sudden twinge in my back. My partner didn't miss a trick, but he also knew I was stubborn as hell.

"You just want to drop more things in my lap," he teased. "First, you send me back to the precinct to work on the Rodriguez angle, and then you call me to pick you up. Do I look like your chauffeur?"

"No. You need one of those little black caps."

He reached for his phone and passed the tattoo verification off to someone else. "You sure, you're okay, Liv? You really ought to get checked out."

"I'm fine." Even as I said the words, I could practically hear Emma lecturing me. "I don't think it was an accident."

"What do you mean?"

"I don't know, but it was weird. Cars don't just stall. The entire electrical system just turned off."

He gave my hand a quick squeeze before reaching for the gearshift. "All that matters is you're okay."

I nodded, lost in thought.

FOURTEEN

"Hey, do you have a few minutes?" I asked.

"I thought you didn't have time for me," ADA Winters said, not bothering to look away from the brief he was reading.

"Things change." I stepped inside and took a seat in front of his desk. "I actually have a favor to ask. Well, maybe a few favors."

He looked up, surprised by my disheveled appearance. "What happened?"

"Nothing." I looked away, but he gently grabbed my chin and forced me to face him. "I got into a car accident."

"Liv." He reached for a bottle of water and poured it onto his handkerchief before pressing it against my still bleeding cut. "This is the DA's office, not a hospital. I think you came to the wrong place."

"No, I didn't. I'm here because I need to get a search warrant signed."

"And you couldn't call the judge yourself?"

"Nope."

"Do I want to know why not?"

"Well, the simple answer is my phone's DOA. I'm guessing it happened in the accident."

Logan's eyes darted into the almost empty hallway, spotting Fennel lingering near the breakroom and chatting with one of the legal secretaries. "And your partner's phone?"

My fingers accidentally brushed against his as I reached for the damp cloth he was still pressing against my eyebrow. "You can stop that now." I took the cloth from him and pulled it away. "See, all better."

He looked sheepish and dropped back into his chair. "Why are you here, Liv?"

"All right, so here's the deal." And I proceeded to tell him about what we found inside the hotel and the tattooed tow truck driver. "It all connects to Axel Kincaid."

"You're probably right, but you've been at this long enough to know that isn't enough."

"That's why I came to see you. I was hoping you'd have a suggestion."

"Get some actual evidence."

"That's what I'm trying to do. Fennel brought Kincaid in for questioning last night. We thought he'd cooperate, but he has powerful friends. And he's been at this long enough that he won't even give an inch."

"What about the partial prints from the bag?"

"Not a match, but he was in the bathroom where the money was stashed. And we found cocaine residue. Can't we finagle these details into something usable?"

"It's not solid enough."

I glanced back out the door. This had been Brad's idea, and I was desperate enough to go along with it. "Yeah, I know. And even if we tricked a judge into signing a warrant, it might get kicked out, along with whatever else we find, because the grounds are so flimsy."

Winters snickered. "Well, if the cop thing doesn't work out, you could always try your hand at law." He probably believed the comment was a compliment rather than an insult. "What were the other favors you wanted?"

"We need a subpoena for Spark's client list. We have grounds. Spark's the only known connection between the two GTA victims, and since one of the car thieves killed a guy, it stands to reason we ought to investigate to the best of our ability."

"That I can do," Logan said. "Why did you wait so long to ask?"

"Kincaid's connected. A lot of powerful people are on his client list, and the department's coming under pressure to look elsewhere for a connection."

"I see." He made a note to draft the paperwork. "You'll have it in the morning."

"I always knew you were good for something."

He waved a finger at me. "This means you owe me, DeMarco." He nodded at Fennel, who was now leaning against the door. "It looks like you have your hands full."

"Don't I know it." Brad met my eyes. "You ready to go, Liv?"

"Actually, I think I'll hang around here for a bit," I looked at Logan, "if that's okay."

"Yeah, no problem."

"Walk me out, DeMarco," my partner insisted, and I got up from the chair, feeling a stiffness in my back that hadn't been there this morning. He waited until we were in the elevator before saying, "It wasn't my intention to pimp you out. You don't have to trade favors. You can say no."

I slapped his arm. "It's not like that, and you know it."

He grinned. "Whatever you say."

"I'm just not ready to go back to the apartment, not after this afternoon. Plus, Kincaid told me to lay low until tomorrow night. I had the surveillance team pulled off the apartment and rerouted to monitor more of Kincaid's crew. I doubt they'd try anything after you raided the club, but y'never know."

"It wasn't much of a raid."

The thought I'd been chasing all afternoon finally coalesced in my mind. "I've been thinking about the hotel. Rodriguez's keycard allowed access to authorized areas and the garage. The maid's keycard granted free reign of the guestrooms. Assuming the two are connected, if the killer had both keycards, he'd have unfettered access to anywhere in the hotel. Inside and out. Mac's checking for anything out of the ordinary, but since Mr. Hart had a room reservation, maybe the thieves stole more than just his car."

"He didn't report anything missing."

"Maybe he couldn't."

Fennel thought about what I said. "You think the contraband in the ceiling is his?"

"I don't know, but the partials on the money didn't match the partials on the outside of the plastic bag. And we don't have Hart's prints on file. If it is his cash, his prints might be on it."

"You know, I like it much better when you aren't banned from the precinct." The elevator doors opened, and Brad stepped out. "I'll add finding a creative way of getting Hart's prints to the list of things I'm working on."

"Hey." I tugged on his arm and pulled him close. No one was around, but I didn't want anyone to overhear what I was about to say. "You know I depend on you. But if something's going on and you need to step away from this, tell me."

"Jesus, Liv," he scrubbed a hand down his face, "it was just a few drinks. I needed to blow off steam after Kincaid got kicked. It's not a problem. I give you my word." He tried to move away, but I grabbed his arm. "What?"

I hugged him. "Thank you."

"For what?"

"Always having my back."

"You need to get your head examined. You might have a concussion or something. That would explain why you're being neurotic."

I stuck my tongue out and watched him walk away. "Drive safe," I called, stepping back inside the elevator. My mind went back to the accident. Images of the totaled car, the sight of the concrete divider inches from me, and the sound of the passenger door crushing beneath the weight of the bus made my heart race.

Clinging to the rail, I needed to get a grip. It was a close call, but it had nothing to do with the job. It had to do with the uncertainty of life. And truth be told, it was the reason I didn't want to go back to the apartment. I didn't want to be alone behind enemy lines. I was tired of undercover work. This began as a sting to root out an underground casino and stop a car thief, and somehow, it turned into two homicides.

When the elevator stopped on the proper floor, I made my way to the ladies' room and splashed some cold water on my face. I could barely keep it together. Who was I to dictate terms, especially to Brad? He'd seen a lot worse than I ever had. I'd probably drink too, but the problem wasn't the drinking. It was when he let it get out of control. It had only happened once that I knew of, but it scared the hell out of me. I never wanted to see him like that again.

After a few deep breaths, I returned to Winters' office. In the interim, he had finished reviewing the brief and cleared his desk. He hoisted a file box on top and smiled at me.

"I ordered dinner."

"Impressive," I retorted.

He smirked. "You ain't seen nothing yet." He took some files out of the box and spread them out, flipping one open. "Duncan Crane used to date an exotic dancer."

My brow furrowed. "I'm getting the strangest sensation of déjà vu. Didn't we already go over this?"

"Yes, but I think Sasha's our best bet."

"Unless Crane's dead." I rubbed my eyes. "A lot of people are turning up dead lately."

Logan ignored the commentary. "Sasha works in a mostly cash business."

"And we suspect she's bankrolling Crane in order to keep him off our radar."

"Right, but that must mean they have to meet up at some point."

"That would make sense, except we've checked her apartment and the titty bar. No Crane. You even had the locals put her under surveillance, but you still didn't come up with anything."

"Some of the dancers entertain at a fleabag motel near the interstate. The owner makes it a point not to pay attention to who comes and goes."

"Do you have any actual evidence, Mr. Assistant District Attorney?"

"Johnny and I went on a little road trip. Thought we'd get the lay of the land."

"Or some other kind of lay," I muttered.

"I think Duncan's there, but I don't have much faith in the locals to locate him or bring him in. They don't seem too interested in helping out."

"You do realize that's out of my jurisdiction. Captain Grayson would have to get approval from local law enforcement to allow me to investigate and apprehend Crane."

"Well, the bench warrant is signed. So there is cause to bring him in."

"Y'know, there are other cops in this city besides me. You have investigators who work from this office. Why can't you get one of them to do it?"

"They think it's a waste of time. They've been to the motel and the strip joint, but they never spotted Duncan, and Sasha claims she hasn't seen him in months. Nothing in her financials suggest otherwise."

"But it's a cash business," I said, seeing where his thoughts were.

"They're going to half-ass it, and if Crane's there, he'll slip away. I need someone who's going to take this seriously."

"I can't go anywhere until I put a killer behind bars. Have you considered a private eye, bounty hunter, or a skip tracer? It's a little unorthodox, but they have a vested interest in delivering."

"Just look through the data I've compiled in the last two days and let me know if it's worth pursuing."

"Yeah, okay." I took the offered file. Logan had taken dozens of surveillance photos at the motel and bar. He also ran the plates of every car in the parking lot. One of the rentals at the motel was registered to Sasha. "Y'know, if the lawyer thing doesn't work out, you might have a career as a cop."

"What can I say? I'm a jack of all trades."

I reviewed his findings, but without any photographic proof or witness corroboration, I still had trouble believing Duncan Crane was alive and in hiding. And if he was in hiding and ADA Winters found him, that probably meant the men he was scheduled to testify against would find him too. This couldn't wait, but if Winters rushed it, Crane might get tipped and disappear again.

"When's he due in court?"

"Two weeks."

"You got everything prepped?"

"Everything except my key witness."

"All right." I thought for a moment. "You need a professional to handle this. You need proof Duncan's there. Whoever you hire needs to maintain eyes on him and needs to make sure no one else is snooping around."

"I'll find someone to sit on the motel, but what do I do once I get verification?"

"We'll get authorization to pick him up, and we'll place him in protective custody until his court date. Depending on what he says, you might have to coordinate with the marshals."

"Yeah, no problem."

I gave Logan a suspicious look. "You didn't need me for any of this. Why the insistence on my stopping by?"

He began placing the files back in the box. "You told me to stick with the ex and to follow the money. I wanted to make sure I was doing it right."

That was a bullshit answer, but before I could call him out on it, our dinner arrived.

FIFTEEN

A few hours after the red blip vanished off the screen, the backup team was pulled off the apartment. For a moment, he allowed himself to relax. Even though Liv DeMarco no longer posed a threat, her brethren would be looking for answers. He couldn't let his guard down. Not yet.

The handcrafted device couldn't be traced, not that they would even know what it was or how it worked. He doubted they recovered it. It was just more wreckage from the crash. He heard about the pile-up when he checked the traffic reports. The local papers plastered a photo of her crushed car on their websites as a breaking story. Although no fatalities were reported, she must be down for the count.

The only thing he regretted was not getting to watch the mayhem. Cars fascinated him, whether they were racing or crashing. But wasn't that what made NASCAR an American pastime?

Burying the thoughts into the darker recesses of his mind, he tucked the gun at the small of his back and pulled his jacket over the top. He didn't button his suit, knowing it would show the telltale bulge.

"Evening, sir," Rick greeted.

He nodded in return and entered Spark. It was early. A few regulars chatted at the bar. He went to the end and ordered a drink. With the bartender occupied, he continued down the hall. The security cameras didn't cover the rear hallway in order to maintain a separation between the club and the private back room.

He went past the sealed door and stepped into the office. Not bothering to turn on the light, he removed the gun from behind his back, carefully wiped it, and placed it in the middle drawer. The police would never find it here.

* * *

"Thanks for the ride and dinner."

"Anytime, Detective." Logan winked. "I'll let you know as soon as I get verification."

"I agree the rental car in Sasha's name appears hinky, but don't get your hopes up."

"Don't worry. I'm still exploring other avenues to make sure the rest of the case is rock solid. But honestly, without Crane, it doesn't look good."

"They might have already gotten to him," I warned. "He might be dead. It's been happening to a lot of people lately."

"Either way, I need to find him."

I stepped out of the car and went up the path to my parents' house. Unlocking the front door, I entered the dark foyer and typed in the security code before the alarm sounded. My parents only set it when they went to bed, and since it was almost eleven, I figured they must have turned in early.

Gunnie barked twice, alerting everyone to the intruder before bolting down the steps and sliding to a stop at my feet.

"Shh," I soothed, scratching behind his ears. He quieted and followed me into the kitchen.

"He's a shitty guard dog," Dad said, startling me.

"Shouldn't you be holding a shotgun or something?" I asked. "What if I was a burglar or rapist?"

"They don't usually get dropped off by ADAs."

"You were spying on me?"

"It's not my fault the car set off the motion sensors and the outside lights." He grinned. "Plus, it doesn't matter how old you get. If a boy drops you off at home, I'm going to check him out."

"It was a work thing."

"Logan Winters is still a boy," Dad insisted. He looked down at the dog. "You and I need to have a talk about your duties in this house. You're expected to earn your keep." Gunnie let out another bark and bumped the pantry with his nose. Dad handed him a treat and took a seat at the table across from me. "What happened to you? Did you try out for the mud wrestling team?"

"I got into a fender bender."

"Did anyone get hurt?"

"Nothing serious."

He nodded. "Good. Did you file the proper paperwork?"

I glared at him. Sometimes, he treated me like a sixteen year old. "Yes, Dad."

He held up his palms. "I was just making sure. You don't want to get jammed up over something stupid." He frowned. "I didn't expect to see you again so soon. Is everything okay, honey?"

"Yeah, fine."

"Something's bothering you. What is it?"

"Nothing."

"Nothing sounds like guy problems or female problems. I'm not necessarily equipped to handle either, but I'll give it a whirl if you want."

"It's this case."

"Did Detective Harding follow through like he was supposed to?"

I shouldn't have asked for the favor. "Yeah, above and beyond, except my CI died due to her injuries. I'm not even sure it's the same killer."

"Fill me in."

"Harding got a description of Becca's killer, but it was too vague to be of any use. The man who attacked my CI wore a dark suit, white shirt, and black tie. The witness said he's tall with dark hair, but she didn't get a look at his face."

"Do the descriptions match?"

I laughed bitterly. "Honestly, it sounds just like my prime suspect, but as usual, he has an alibi."

"And you can't break it?"

"It's not that simple. The girl who saw him attack Becca was blitzed out of her mind. Harding said she won't come forward, and even if she did, it wouldn't matter."

"Unreliable witness. I'm guessing she's in the business."

"Yeah."

Dad thought for a moment. "Any other way to get this guy? What about the cars? Only a handful of thieves know how to make custom imports vanish without a trace. Have you checked to see what crews are operating locally?"

"As far as we can tell, no one local can pull off a job like that, except Axel Kincaid, but it's not enough. I just had a long talk with ADA Winters, and we need more."

"Tell me what you got," Dad insisted, so I told him about the missing cars, the tow truck driver, the hotel, and Axel Kincaid and his crew. "Sounds complicated and potentially dangerous. You have backup?"

"Fennel's doing everything he can through the official channels, and a team's been sitting on my cover apartment, just to make sure everything remains copacetic. I'll probably be wired tomorrow night when I meet with Kincaid. So we're doing it by the book, but Kincaid's extremely careful. Without his prints or evidence linking directly to him or Spark, we can't get a judge to sign off on anything."

"And since half the judges are club members, it makes it even more complicated." Dad licked his lips. "Grayson's probably getting a lot of flak over this."

"He is, but we're moving forward anyway. It started as a vice investigation which turned into a string of GTAs and now two homicides. It's too big. It can't be brushed under the rug. We have to shut it down."

"You will, but don't rush it. You're dealing with dangerous men. You can't afford a misstep."

Gunnie let out a whimper and wagged his tail, bumping his nose against the cabinet again. I raised an eyebrow. "You hiding a dame in there?"

"No, just his biscuits," Mom said. She went to the cabinet and gave the dog a treat. "I thought I heard your voice." She gave me a hug and kissed the top of my head. "Are you staying the night, sweetie?"

"If that's okay."

"It's always okay." She narrowed her eyes. "How did that happen? Or do I even want to know?"

"Fender bender," Dad said.

"And you didn't call to tell us." Mom made a tsk noise. "Olive, we're your parents. We need to know these things." She gave me another hug. "I'll go make up your bed." She looked pointedly at the clock. "You need to get some rest. You look tired."

"In a few minutes," Dad insisted.

"Hold him to that," she told me.

"Thanks, Mom. I love you."

SIXTEEN

I rested my forehead against the shower wall while the hot water cascaded down my back and relieved the tension in my muscles. I should turn the water off. The planet had enough problems without me wasting natural resources. But I didn't move from that spot until the water ran cold.

Reluctantly, I shut it off and reached for a towel. The smell of my father's homemade sausage patties wafted through the vent and made my stomach growl. After dressing and drying my hair, I went down to the kitchen to find Brad helping himself to a heaping pile of scrambled eggs.

"What the hell are you doing here?" I grabbed a mug from the cabinet and reached for the coffeepot.

"Picking up your sorry ass," Brad teased. On second thought, he cast a quick glance at my father, wondering if my parents would think his comment was out of line. My partner cringed and gave me a worried look, but I laughed it off. My parents were used to a lot worse from my friends. "I got you something. It's in the car."

"Ooh, a present." I grabbed a plate and loaded it up with eggs, sausage, and fresh fruit. "Is it Spark's client list?"

"No, that's at the station. The captain already assigned a team to go through Kincaid's records." Brad put the fork down and reached for the plate of sausage. He took one, cut it in half, and slipped a piece to Gunnie. "At least Winters came through."

"He said he would."

"But he's a lawyer," Brad said around a mouthful. "They lie for a living."

"Don't we all?"

"Liv," Brad said in an all too familiar tone, and I gave him a sharp look.

His tone set off my mom's radar or killer instincts since she appeared from out of nowhere and joined us at the table. "Is everything okay, sweetie?"

"Yeah. We just have a long day ahead of us. And a long night. We should probably get going. Brad's sorry for eating you out of house and home and interrupting your morning routine."

"Nonsense." Mom beamed at my partner. "You're welcome here anytime, Bradley. And don't forget about dinner."

"No, ma'am." Brad swallowed a final bite and brought his plate to the sink. He rinsed it, loaded it into the dishwasher, and offered his hand to my father. "Thanks for breakfast, Captain DeMarco."

Dad shook his hand. "It's Vince."

"Yes, sir." Brad looked absolutely starstruck. "Vince."

I looked at my mom and rolled my eyes. *Men*, I mouthed. She laughed and told us to have a nice day. I grabbed my bag, said goodbye to my dad, gave Gunnie a final scratch behind the ears, and met Brad at the car.

"So what did you get me?" I asked. He reached into the back seat and handed me a paper bag. "A new cell phone."

"It's just a burner. I already activated it. You're gonna need it, especially since you're going to be alone with Kincaid. I had your number transferred, so you're good to go."

I dug through the bag, finding something else. "You bought me chocolate."

"Don't start."

I held up the treat. "But you did."

"I had to stop at three places just to find your damn organic chocolate. You better be worth it."

Even though we just finished breakfast, I unwrapped the bar and broke off a square and gave it to him. "Thanks."

"It's our ritual. I can't let you risk your life on an op without getting you a treat."

I swallowed, folding the wrapper over the candy bar and tucking it into my purse. "You think Kincaid is going to try to kill me?"

"He might have already tried once." He watched me from the corner of his eye. "Mac and a few of the crime techs examined the device found at the scene of the accident. They think it's what caused your car to stall."

"Do you think Kincaid planted it?"

"We have no way of knowing who, but someone put it there."

"And Axel dropped by my apartment the other day." I stared out the windshield. "Does the captain know I'm blown?"

"We don't know—"

"Yes, we do. This asshole sent us a warning, but we didn't listen. So he came for me. He's getting more brazen."

Fennel turned to look at me. "Say the word and we'll pull the plug. We'll find another way of getting this guy."

"No. Axel has something planned for me tonight. I want to find out what it is."

"Fine, but you're wearing a wire. Backup teams will maintain eyes on you. I will be with them. Just utter the safe word, and I will bust in and beat his ass." Fennel maneuvered into a reserved space at the hotel and cut the engine. "Since Kincaid's lawyer has positioned himself at the precinct, this is our staging ground."

We entered and returned to the suite. Several members of our unit were set up inside. Captain Grayson convinced Mr. Hart to come back for a follow-up interview in the hopes of getting his prints. It wouldn't be too hard to dust the coffee cup or water bottle after the man left. And it would be easier than trying to force him to comply.

The hotel cameras proved useless. According to the footage, no unauthorized personnel accessed any restricted parts of the hotel. Of course, it was possible someone had dressed like hotel staff to avoid being noticed or simply maneuvered through the blind spots, but conjecture and speculation wouldn't get us anywhere.

Despite our best efforts, we still hadn't identified the tow truck driver either. By the time the department sent someone else to speak to the tattoo artist, the shop was closed. We had an all-points out on the tow truck. A patrol unit thought they spotted it early this morning, but it was a false alarm.

"Hey, did Fennel tell you?" Mac asked as soon as she entered the hotel room.

"Tell me what?" I glanced at my partner who was

leaning over a workstation and staring at the hotel lobby feed from the day of the shooting.

"We have a mock-up of the tow truck driver's tattoo." She rifled through a folder and pulled out a printout. "It's a grim reaper holding an upside-down scythe."

"You're sure about this?" The only visible portion had been the curved blade of the scythe.

"Mostly. Just keep in mind, it's a rough approximation." She pointed to the large upper portion of the tattoo. "This part might not match exactly, but I did what I could."

"How?"

"It took a lot of work, but after playing with the levels for hours, I was able to make out the dark ink behind the dude's white sleeve. With a little guesswork, the computer filled in the missing pieces."

I took the folder from her and flipped through the pages. It didn't get any hits in the prison database. Was it possible the car thief didn't have a record? Most offenders had priors which meant the tattoo was fairly new.

I reached for a tablet someone abandoned and did a search. "Yesterday, I made a list of tattoo artists in the city with a similar style, but now that we know what the rest of the image is, we can probably narrow it further." I graced Mac with an appreciative smile. "Good work."

"Thanks."

After some research and a few calls, I found the tattoo artist. Strangely enough, his name had been the first one on my list. Too bad I didn't make it to my destination yesterday. By now, the bastard might be in custody.

"Let's take a ride, Fennel."

Brad drove to the tattoo parlor, and we spoke to the

artist, Kai Kahale. Kai recognized the rudimentary approximation of his work and plucked half a dozen photographs off the wall to show us. "It could be any of these. They all feature the same blade in that position," Kai said.

"Impressive," Brad remarked. "We're going to need your clients' information."

Kai nodded and went to the front desk. "The last one I did was six months ago." He squinted at the labels on the folders until he found what he was looking for. Kai's face sagged. "Oh." He spun the page with the attached receipt around and pointed. "That's his name and contact info."

Brad read the name. "John Smith. 555-1234. This guy thinks he's cute." He glowered at Kai. "You didn't think that was strange?"

"I just write down what they tell me. The only time I worry is when a kid comes in. They have to be eighteen to get inked, so I check IDs in those instances. Other than that, I don't pay much attention."

"What about the receipt?" I asked. This had to be our guy, but I took copies of the other five customers' information who received similar tattoos, just in case. We'd have to check them all out.

Brad tore the receipt off the page. "It's only the last four digits of a credit card, but we might be able to work with it." While my partner phoned in the information to see if we could get an actual name and address for John Smith, I questioned Kai.

"Do you remember what John Smith looked like?"

Kai bit his bottom lip. "Not really. I ink a lot of people." He examined the photographs hanging on a corkboard and plucked two more off. Unlike the other photos he handed me, these included the person's face, not just the tattoo. "I like to keep copies of my work, but not everyone lets me take a picture when I'm finished. These two did. The tattoo you're looking for is similar."

"But neither of these men is John Smith?" I asked.

Kai read the dates on the bottom. "No, I'm sorry."

I studied the men in the photos, recognizing something familiar about them, but I couldn't put my finger on it. One was blond, and the other appeared too lanky to be our suspect, but it wouldn't hurt to run them through facial recognition. "We'll need to hold on to these."

"That's fine. Whatever I can do to help."

I tucked the photos into a folder with the other forms. "What about what Mr. Smith drove? Do you remember his car?"

Kai snorted. "I have no idea."

I looked around, but I didn't spot any security cameras. "Did he say or do anything strange? Anything you can tell me about this guy will be a help."

"He was white. And if I'm remembering correctly, I'm pretty sure it was his first tattoo."

"Do you remember how old he was?"

"Over eighteen," Kai said.

"No shit."

He held up his palms. "I dunno. In his thirties, I think. I just remember thinking it was strange he waited so long to get a tattoo. Most people get their first one when they're in their early twenties. So he had to be older than that."

"Would you take a look at some photos and let me know if anyone rings a bell?" I opened the file containing intel on Kincaid and his crew and removed a stack of glossies.

Kai flipped through them but didn't pick anyone out. Either he didn't remember what the tow truck driver looked like, or he wasn't part of Kincaid's crew. My thoughts returned to my earlier conclusion – we were dealing with two crews. Two separate sets of crimes, but the man with the tattoo connected to both. I flipped through the information Kai had given me a second time. Who the hell was John Smith?

"Yeah, okay, thanks." Brad hung up the phone, and I looked expectantly at him. "You're never gonna believe this."

A feeling of dread filled me. "What?"

"It was a prepaid credit card. Someone is checking to see if the owner registered it or logged in to check the balance. If not, they'll do what they can to determine where it was purchased," Brad said.

I rubbed both hands down my face. "Son of a bitch." I circled the room, frustrated and angry. We didn't even know enough to know how involved the tow truck driver was, but considering how far he went to conceal his identity, he had to be involved in something shady. He was at the hotel two hours before the heist. He was in on it.

"Thanks for your time." Brad handed Kai a card. "If you remember anything else or if Smith comes back, give me a call."

Kai nodded and tucked the card away.

On the way back to the hotel, I got a call from the lab. They matched the DNA found beneath Becca's fingernails to Fox. "Send uniforms to pick him up," I instructed.

SEVENTEEN

"Are you sure about this, DeMarco?" Fennel paced back and forth as the techs performed a soundcheck. "We linked one of Kincaid's guys to the pro's murder. He's in custody. We'll break him. He's facing murder charges. He'll roll."

"You don't know Fox." When he left the bar, he must have tracked down Becca to find out why we were together. I never should have left the bar with her. It was stupid. A rookie mistake. And one I would regret the rest of my life. "He won't crack."

Brad blew into his fist. "Where's Axel taking you?"

"I don't know." I bit my lip. "I don't know what he has planned." I checked my gun, made sure the safety was on, and tucked it away. Better safe than sorry.

"We'll leapfrog. Two mobile units will maintain eyes. We'll set up better once you reach your destination."

"Don't get spotted," I warned.

The techs finished with the equipment, and Brad turned to them. "Give us the room." After they departed, he said, "Fox's on to you. He has to be. It stands to reason he probably sabotaged your car. He must have told Kincaid. You might be walking into a trap."

"Then be ready to move in as soon as Kincaid tips his hand. I don't care how we get him, but we get him, even if it's on some bullshit charge like threatening a police officer. We just need enough to get inside his club and find out what's really going on."

"I got your back, Liv. Just don't do anything stupid."

"You know me."

"Hence the warning."

A taxi dropped me off near my cover apartment, and I walked the rest of the way, not wanting to tip off Axel in case he was keeping tabs on me. Did Becca sell me out? I spoke to Axel after Fox got to her, and he seemed convinced of my loyalty. But it could have been an act. Despite the way it appeared, I still didn't know how much Axel or his crew knew. The only thing we were sure of was someone sabotaged my car.

The apartment remained untouched, and I made certain everything was still safely filed away. No one had been here. The nervous energy coursed through me, sending little jolts of adrenaline into my system. Any minute now.

I watched the clock, growing increasingly impatient as the seconds ticked by. It was 12:30. Kincaid said he'd pick me up around midnight. He was late.

"Still no sign of Axel," I said, knowing Fennel would hear me through the radio. "Does anyone know his current location?"

My phone rang, and I picked it up. "He's at Spark."

"All right. I'm heading over there."

"Liv," Fennel said, "that's not the plan."

"Neither is dying of old age."

He let out a disgruntled groan and disconnected. Since I was sans car, I grabbed my helmet and hopped on my bike. Ten minutes later, I went to the side entrance and stared up at the camera. George buzzed me through without hesitation, and I tucked my helmet in the locker room before making my way into the club.

Axel was in his office; the phone pressed to his ear. I knocked gently on the door, and he looked up from the paperwork scattered on his desk. He held up a finger, indicating I should wait, and searched through his top drawer for something. I leaned against the doorjamb.

"Yeah, fine. I expect a delivery tomorrow afternoon, or I will find another supplier." He slammed the phone down. "Shit." For a moment, he looked completely confused to see me. "What are you doing here?"

"Did we get our signals crossed?"

"Oh," he blinked, "we had plans." He shook off his confusion.

I jerked my chin at the phone. "What's that about?"

"The liquor delivery was delayed, and time got away from me." He grabbed his jacket. "Is that what you're wearing?"

"You told me to dress comfortably, but I can go home and change."

He studied my jeans and button-up blouse. "It's fine. We're already late. Let's go."

"Where are we going?" I asked as he guided me out of his office and down the rear hallway to the side exit.

"You'll see." He held the door, waiting for me to exit. Parked at the rear of the building was a burnt orange Maserati. I couldn't help but wonder if it was the same one he'd taken for a joy ride that vanished into thin air.

"This is yours?" The color would make it much easier for the follow cars to maintain a visual, but the engine might pose a problem.

"Do you like it?"

"It's gorgeous."

"Just wait until you see what she can do." He peeled away from the curb, checking the mirrors constantly. "It's about time you learn what my business is really about, Ms. Bell."

The use of my cover name set off my cop instincts. "Where are we going?"

"I can't tell you. I don't want to ruin the surprise." He approached the next traffic light, slowing to a crawl even though the light was green. It would be red by the time we got to it. He must know he was being followed. The mobile units would end up right on his tail. One of them passed us, turning and pulling to a stop. The other joined the row of cars angrily honking behind us. When the light turned yellow, he gunned the engine, shooting through just as it turned red.

"What the hell are you doing?"

"Making sure we have our privacy."

"Paranoid much?"

He knew. He fucking knew. But I was too stubborn to end this, so I played along, calling his bluff.

"What is much?" He darted through traffic easily, gaining speed and accelerating until we hit the interstate.

"I didn't realize we were crossing state lines. Where are we going? Canada?" At least the team knew we were northbound on the interstate.

"You ask a lot of questions, Liv."

"Well, you've never needed me for something outside of Spark before. I want to be prepared."

When we were no longer in the city, he pulled off the interstate. "Trust me. You'll want to see this. I imagine it's what you've been waiting for." He zipped around the curves of the small town roads as if he'd made this drive a hundred times. After crossing beneath another traffic light, four cars pulled horizontally across the road behind us, blocking the street. The mobile units would be made the second they arrived. Kincaid wanted me isolated. My fingers tightened around my purse.

"Where the hell are we?"

Axel didn't answer, and I edged farther away. My hand slipped into my bag.

"Answer me."

He pointed out the windshield. "Look." Bright streetlights and storefronts chased away the dark, and I saw dozens, maybe even hundreds, of exotic sports cars.

"What is this place? Where are we?"

He chuckled, sensing my uneasiness and taking pleasure in my anxiety. "We're pretending to be extras in a car racing flick."

"You're going to race this car?"

"No. Tonight, we're just watching." He pulled to a stop near a few other cars. "I didn't set this up. I just heard about it. As you know, Spark's clientele has eclectic tastes. They enjoy the natural high from living on the edge. And they are wealthy. We don't buy cars like this to leave them in the garage and collect dust. They're meant to race, and as with any competition, there's always wagering."

"This is what you organize in the back room?"

Kincaid tore his eyes from the four vehicles lining up at the white line to look at me. "Without permits and authorization, a venture like this would be illegal."

"Did you set this up?" I repeated.

"Shh, it's about to start."

In the blink of an eye, four cars raced past, almost like a scene out of a summer blockbuster, but this wasn't a quarter mile. I didn't know how long the course was, but when a blue Porsche returned to the starting point, I knew it was over. We watched a few groups get out and cluster around the car, money was exchanged, and the area cleared.

A second set of cars approached the white line, and Axel lost interest and turned to face me. "It's not a particularly exciting spectator sport, but as you can see, I have no need for additional vehicles. I already have plenty of my own. And I doubt anyone from my club is hurting for a new ride either." He jerked his chin back at the windshield, encouraging me to look around. "I don't see any yellow Ferrari or silver McLarens. The police won't find what they're looking for here."

Shit. "Do you race?"

He shrugged. The bastard knew it was best not to tip his hand. He would admit nothing.

"Why the hell did you want to show me this?"

Axel's cold eyes bore into me. "This is the reason the police believe I'm involved in those two GTAs. So I wanted you to see what goes on. I don't set up these races. I'm not responsible for the illegal betting, the public endangerment, or the traffic violations. But I know about this, and I know a lot of Spark's members enjoy these races. That doesn't make us thieves or murderers. No one gets hurt. The roads are blocked off. It's a tiny sleepy town. We make sure there aren't any accidents."

"We?"

He smoldered. "They. He. Whoever's in charge."

You. But I didn't voice it.

"Why did you bring me here?"

"You know why."

Something was going on, and I turned my attention back to what was happening beyond the windshield. "Who's the guy with the reaper tattoo?" He appeared to be in charge of taking bets. Typically, the house wins, but our tow truck driver seemed more like a three-time loser. At least I finally found the son of a bitch, but I wasn't in a position to do anything about it.

"They call him Marvin," Kincaid replied.

"Is he a member of Spark?"

Axel shook his head.

"Do you know anything else about Marvin? Does Marvin have a last name?"

"I'm sure he does." Axel was infuriating.

"Do you know what it is?"

"No."

We fell silent as more bets were placed, and two tricked out cars approached the spray-painted line. A scantily clad woman stood between the two cars, shimmied her panties down her legs, and held them high in the air before waving them like a flag. The cars took off.

"I thought you said your clientele was classy," I remarked.

"What do you expect from startup punks who spent their formative years locked in their mothers' basements, playing video games?"

The cars disappeared from sight. A rumble of cheering sounded, and Marvin the tow truck driver began taking more bets on the sidelines. Axel put the car in gear and took the back streets, waiting for the four cars that sealed us in to let us out.

"I hope you found this enlightening, Detective."

My eyes went to him, but he stared at the road ahead. I had a million questions, but asking them now did not seem like the best plan. "What are you talking about?"

His gaze snapped to me for just a moment. "Don't lie to me, Liv. I know who you are."

"How long have you known?"

He snorted, refusing to answer.

By the time we made it back to the city, two mobile units were waiting outside Spark. Axel glared at me. Apparently, he thought our little field trip would make the PD back off the investigation. Instead, the police were out in force. They didn't take kindly to one of their own being isolated from the support team.

"Busy night, Mr. Kincaid?" Fennel asked.

"What the hell do you want now? I have nothing to say." Axel stared at me. "I gave you a gift. Call off the hounds."

"I can't do that."

"We have a search warrant," Brad said.

Kincaid ripped the paper from Fennel's hand. "On what grounds?"

"One of your employees was arrested for murder earlier today. We need access to his workspace, and since his official title is general manager, the judge granted us clearance to search your entire club."

Axel grimaced and reached for his phone. "I'm calling my lawyer."

Fennel ignored him and entered the establishment. "You okay?" he whispered.

I nodded. "The tow truck driver was there."

"We know. We've set up roadblocks. Whenever they disband, we'll ID his tattoo and scoop him up."

"You're not going to shut down the races?"

"It's out of our jurisdiction. We notified the locals, but I'm guessing they already know about it. The mayor recently received a large anonymous donation to his campaign fund. I suspect its hush money to look the other way."

"This is unbelievable."

"Money talks, DeMarco." He jerked his chin at Kincaid. "Case in point." Fennel moved through the main room, checking the sofa cushions and glancing at the speakers.

"If you find any spare change, you can keep it," Axel said, "unless you're afraid someone might construe that as a bribe."

Brad ignored the dig and looked behind the bar and in the kitchen. "Mind if I look in here?" He pointed to the door to the back room.

"Knock yourself out," Axel said. "It's not like I could stop you anyway."

The back room held nothing but some hexagonal tables surrounded by chairs. A few bar carts, serving trays, and extra stools stood in the corner. It didn't look nearly as fabulous as it did on the nights he used it to allegedly run his poker games or set up the races. That's probably why vice never got anywhere on the underground casino front. Kincaid made an effort to keep things neat and tidy. He probably suspected a police raid every night. Or most nights. He probably knew all along he had a cop in his midst. It was no wonder our case had been subverted.

Fennel crouched down, probably looking for lost poker chips, but came up empty.

"Are you done, Detective? Or do you want to volunteer to clean the bathrooms? The floors could use a good scrubbing." Axel was getting impatient. My gut said he was nervous. I just wasn't sure why.

Fennel approached the office in the back. He reached in and flipped on the light. Brad checked the shelves, the closet, and the desk. When he opened the middle drawer, he smiled. "I suppose you have a permit for this?" He hooked the handgun on the end of his pen and held it up. "It looks like a forty caliber.

The same type used to kill Juan Rodriguez."

"That isn't mine," Axel insisted.

"This is your office, right?" Fennel glanced at the nameplate on the door.

"Yes, but most of my employees have access to it."

"In that case, who left the gun in your office?"

Kincaid narrowed his eyes at the weapon. "I don't know, but I will find out." He sneered at us. "How do I know you didn't plant that while I was gone?"

"Tell it to the judge," I muttered.

Brad stepped closer. "Axel Kincaid you're under arrest. Let's see you get out of this one." He passed Axel off to the uniform who read him his rights. At least we finally had the bastard in custody. He wouldn't slip away again.

EIGHTEEN

No prints were found on the gun. Ballistics had yet to come back, but if it was a match to the slugs we pulled out of Juan Rodriguez, we'd finally be able to put this case behind us. Axel Kincaid wasn't stupid, and I didn't think he'd leave the murder weapon out in the open. But he was arrogant. Still, to leave the gun in his desk with his office door open was just sloppy. Maybe he forgot. Maybe he didn't care. Or maybe he figured under the circumstances, he could claim someone else entered his office and left it. No matter how I twisted the facts, they didn't make a lot of sense.

"We have Fox in the box." Grayson grinned. "Damn, I could be the next Dr. Seuss."

"Yes, you could."

"You want to take a crack at him, DeMarco?"

I pushed away from my desk. "Yeah, thanks." Brad fell into step beside me, and we entered the interrogation room.

Fox looked like he might be sick. "I should have fucking known. Selling drugs my ass. Despite that cop stink, you spent a lot of nights in that cage." He grinned evilly. "Bet it got you off, didn't it? You liked being helpless and locked up for once."

Brad stepped forward. "Watch your mouth. You're speaking to a lady."

"Some lady. I'd say she's more of a c—" His attorney nudged him hard, and he fell silent.

I took a seat across from him. "Things don't look good for you. We found your DNA beneath Becca's fingernails. She got a hold of you, didn't she? Is that why you took the crowbar to her skull?"

"I didn't hit her," Fox said.

Fennel flipped open the ME's report and plucked out the photographs, placing them on the table in front of Fox. "You did more than hit her."

"I told you. I didn't do this." Fox shoved the photos away and turned to stare at the wall.

"Well, she scratched you, so you better tell us how that happened," Brad said.

Fox glanced at his attorney, who nodded. "It's not what it looks like." He blew out a breath.

"Becca was a fighter. If you hadn't overpowered her, she probably would have done a lot worse than scratch you," I said.

"I know who she was." Fox's eye twitched. "She didn't scratch me like that. She must have dug her nails into my back." He exhaled slowly. "We had sex. After I dropped Emilio off at home, I spotted Becca near her usual corner. You said you sold her an eight ball, so I figured she might want to party. She denied it when I asked, but since I had nowhere else to be, I figured what the hell."

"How romantic," I muttered.

"I didn't kill her," Fox insisted. "When I left, she was alive and two hundred bucks richer."

"What time was that?" Brad asked.

Fox thought for a moment. "Around 1:30. Maybe 2:00."

"Where'd you do the deed?" I asked.

"The back seat of my car."

"Did you see anyone else nearby?" I asked. "Did you see Becca with anyone when you were leaving?"

"No. She got out of the car, and I drove off. That was it." He stared at me. "I didn't fucking kill her."

"Did she tell you I was a cop?"

Fox chuckled. "You're shitting me, right? I didn't know you were a pig until the second you stepped foot in this room."

"I need to talk to you outside for a sec," I said to my partner. We excused ourselves and went into the hallway. "Has his vehicle been searched?"

"It's already been impounded, and we searched his apartment. No signs of a struggle. No traces of blood."

"Let's make sure those scratch marks are on his back, and let's get someone to canvass his building and find out if anyone remembers what time he got home that night."

"On it." Brad strode down the hall.

Ducking back into interrogation, I finished with Fox and asked one final question. "Did Axel Kincaid ever say anything to you about Rebecca Johnson?"

"Just that I should stay away from her."

"Why?"

Fox shrugged. "How should I know? Axel has rules for everything."

"Becca told me a story. It sounded like Axel was running girls. Do you know anything about that? Maybe Becca was one of his girls."

"If she was, that's news to me. And I should have gotten a discount."

Disgusted, I left the room. While mulling over the possibilities, I watched the parade of Spark's clientele entering the precinct. I had yet to confront Axel, but he had a list a mile long of witnesses to alibi him out. Furthermore, since the gun was found in his club and he claimed anyone could have placed it, we now had to question everyone who had been inside since the shooting. This was ridiculous, but Axel had clout. Even though it was my investigation, he was pulling the strings.

The desk phone rang, and I grabbed it. Ballistics came back. The gun in Kincaid's desk drawer was a match to the weapon used to kill Juan Rodriguez. We finally had our smoking gun.

"Son of a bitch." Tired of being jerked around, I barked, "Where's Kincaid?"

"Interrogation room three," the sergeant said.

Barging inside, I stared at the smug asshole with the permanent smirk etched on his face. "Something funny?"

"Not in the least, Detective." Kincaid gestured at the empty chair. "I've been waiting for someone to speak to me. I just didn't realize it would be you."

Unlike Fox's attorney, the man in the three thousand dollar suit didn't appear to give a fuck about any of this. Perhaps, it was beneath him, but more than likely, it was because Kincaid called the shots. The lawyer was just here to mop up the potential fallout.

"Tell me why you were at the hotel four days ago," I insisted.

"I had a meeting."

"In the bathroom?"

Kincaid shook his head. "It was canceled."

"Who were you meeting?"

Kincaid leaned forward and rested his palms on the table. "I don't see how that is any of your business."

"You can't come up with a name because it's

bullshit." I narrowed my eyes, watching him for any tics or twitches, but Axel was cool as a cucumber. "We matched the gun from your office to the one used to kill Juan Rodriguez."

"I don't know Juan Rodriguez."

"He was a parking attendant at the hotel. You shot him at point-blank range, and then you stole a car. Ring any bells?"

"Why the fuck would I steal a car? A few hours ago, you were beside me in one of my cars. Why the hell would I need or want another car?"

"Maybe you got tired of the color or wanted something else Italian."

He grinned, a slight chuckle escaping. "I definitely want something else Italian, Detective DeMarco, but it isn't a yellow Ferrari."

Slamming my palm against the table, I circled, watching his reflection in the two-way mirror. "Why were you in the hotel? We're going to figure it out, but if you cooperate, things will go a lot easier for you."

"I told you. I had a meeting. It was canceled at the last minute, and I left. I went straight to Spark, and I didn't leave again until the following morning. We've already gone over this. Your partner already asked me about this the first time he dragged me down here." He scooted closer to the table. "Don't you think if I killed a man and stole a half a million dollar sports car that I would have had to take a detour to hide the car or get rid of the gun?"

"You wiped the gun and left it in your desk drawer. You brought it back to Spark, and since that's the only place you went after the murder and heist, your supposed explanation just makes you look guiltier."

Kincaid fought to keep his anger in check, but the interrogation affected him. "How stupid do you think I am?" His lawyer tucked the phone away and put a hand on Axel's forearm, a silent warning to shut up.

I stared into his eyes. "I'm not sure."

"Then where did I hide the car you think I stole?" Kincaid asked. "Have you found that yet? Wouldn't you need that and some sort of evidence in order to make these ridiculous claims stick?"

The attorney cleared his throat, but Axel pretended not to notice. He was on a roll, so I let him continue. He'd bury himself eventually.

"It's circumstantial at best. I didn't shoot anyone. You haven't located the car. I didn't know Juan Rodriguez, so I don't have a motive. And here's the biggest question of all. Why would I help you with your investigation if I was to blame?"

"Help me?" I practically choked. "You think this is helpful?"

He leaned back. The smirk reappeared on his face. "I knew damn well who you were, and I showed you the illegal car races and the gambling anyway. I even helped identify some of the people involved. I cooperated with your investigation, and you turned around and accused me of murder. That isn't very nice."

"Stop playing me."

"Oh, I'd like nothing more than to play with you, but this isn't how I play. I didn't kill anyone, and I'm not responsible for the GTAs. I have no motive. If I wanted a bright yellow car, I would have bought one. I wouldn't have to steal it. I'm not that kid from the streets. Not anymore. I'm a man with a thriving business and a nine-figure bank account. You have my financials. You know it's true. So unless you have something else, I'll be walking out that door soon enough."

"What about Rebecca Johnson?"

"The prostitute?" Axel snorted. "Seriously, what is

this? Next, you're going to accuse me of jaywalking."

"Was she one of your girls?"

"Oh, so now I run a prostitution ring too? Is that my main focus, or are cars still my thing?" He glared. "The PD needs to get its act together. I'm not the devil, Liv, but I do have a time-share in hell. The weather's usually lovely this time of year. You should go there. My treat."

Mr. Almeada, the attorney, cleared his throat. "To clarify, that was sarcasm. Not a confession."

"Yeah, I got that."

NINETEEN

This was taking too long. He checked his watch. The police were intentionally dragging their feet. He didn't have time for this. In twenty minutes, the device would detonate. He set the timer hours ago to coordinate precisely with the security update. It was his only window of opportunity, or else, he'd have to wait another month. And that wasn't an option when he already had the cars in his possession and transport secured on a cargo ship. Everything was ready. If only they hadn't found the gun in the desk drawer.

He watched the police officers stroll past the room. They weren't in a rush, and they didn't care if anyone else was. He exhaled, closing his eyes and forcing his mind to relax. His partners didn't get caught during the police roundup, so they would be at the hotel to take care of business. The plan was in motion. This was precisely why they had fail-safes in place.

He couldn't have asked for a more perfect alibi than being inside a police station, but he would have preferred the thrill of the front lines. It irked him. This was his plan. He masterminded it. He found the buyers, arranged for the removal and transportation, and now he was stuck here, breathing in the stale air. A cross between a coffee shop and a locker room. He regretted not getting to see it all come to fruition. But his presence would clear him of all suspicion in the eyes of the law. Maybe it was for the best.

He turned his head and watched her through the open door as she stormed down the hall. She was angry, which he found oddly arousing. Truthfully, he was relieved she wasn't dead. It meant he had a chance to spend some quality time with her before their game came to an end and he disappeared for good.

*   *   *

"Where are we on locating the white SUV?" I asked the moment Brad returned to the bullpen.

"It's not in Axel's garage. There's no record of him owning or leasing such a vehicle. And none of the SUVs he owns have been repainted. We didn't find anything with Fox either. But we did find a recent charge in Spark's account to a rental agency. Apparently, the club rented a white SUV last week for a few hours."

"That doesn't help us, unless we can place it at the hotel or prove Kincaid accessed it around the time of the heist." I considered various ways Axel might have been able to gain access to the vehicle again, but none were particularly feasible. "Dammit."

"He's a car thief, Liv. It stands to reason he'd know how to get a car and how to make it disappear."

"We need to identify his accomplices. At least two other men were involved in the heist. I want to know who they are."

"We're working on it," Brad promised. "Marvin Struthers, the tow truck driver, got scooped up late last night when he was leaving the race. Captain Grayson is speaking to him, but from what we can tell, he's nothing more than a repo man."

"A repo man who stole a different SUV the same night the hotel got hit. He's no repo man." I glanced at the captain's darkened office. "He was at the hotel the same time Kincaid was. He's involved."

"That's why Grayson's conducting the interview personally. We have quite a bit on Mr. Struthers since we picked him up after the races, but he actually had paperwork documenting the repossession of the SUV he towed away. He's claiming he didn't steal it. He was just doing his job."

"Where is it now?" I asked.

"In a private lot."

"I thought the stolen SUV belonged to a car service."

"It did, but the owners got into a financial mess and put a few of their vehicles up as collateral against a loan. When the loan came due and they couldn't pay, Struthers picked up the SUV."

"So he isn't a car thief?"

"It doesn't appear so, but like you said, he was at the hotel around the same time Kincaid was. And he's involved with the underground racing. He's connected, somehow."

I reached for Spark's member list, but Marvin Struthers wasn't on it. Kincaid told me he wasn't a member, and given Struthers' blue-collar job, I doubted he would be. But still, there was overlap that couldn't be explained away.

Grabbing Kincaid's phone records, I scanned for any calls or messages between the two. Still nothing.

"Did Kincaid's ISP hand over his internet activity yet?"

"It just came in an hour ago," Fennel said. "I barely had a chance to scan it, but I didn't spot anything out of the ordinary."

I read through Axel's recent e-mail correspondence, hoping something would pop. But it didn't. "What are we missing?"

Fennel sighed. "I don't know. The follow-up with Hart didn't yield any positive results either. We did get a four-point match between his prints and a partial on one of the stacks of cash, but it's not enough to be conclusive."

"What do the techs think?"

"The money probably belongs to Hart, but the partial was too small to be a match to anyone because it was on the edge of the bills."

I drummed my nails on the desk. "Does Hart own a white SUV?"

"You think he hired someone to steal his car?"

"I don't know. All I know is the same SUV was used to dump Becca at the hospital, which means there has to be evidence inside. We have to find the SUV or the stolen cars. Without them, this is going to be a wash. And Kincaid will walk."

"But we have the gun," Brad insisted.

"Yeah," I watched Axel's attorney stride out of the room and into our breakroom to grab a bottle of water, "but something tells me it isn't enough."

Brad picked up the phone. "I'll see if narcotics has made any large coke busts lately or if they know about any dealers working near the hotel. Maybe they can explain why there is cocaine residue in the ceiling."

While he followed up, I reread Hart's statement and ran a background check. Hart didn't own a white SUV either. Reaching for Spark's member list, I started at the top. Someone on this list had to own a white SUV. And I would be damned if it wasn't the same white SUV the killer drove.

"You son of a bitch." I got up and went back into the interrogation room, shoving a pad of paper and pen in front of Axel. "Employee names and contact information. Now."

He cocked his head up at me. "You could say please." After a brief staring contest, he picked up the pen. "Shouldn't you already have this information? You've been on the inside for three months. You know who works at my club. You know their names. Hell, Liv, I thought they were your friends." He continued writing, seemingly taking his time to think about the fifty or so people he employed. "Is this how you treat your friends?" He pushed the pad across the table. "Y'know, if anyone has a right to be pissed, it's me. You betrayed me. It wasn't the other way around."

"You're not the victim here. Stop perverting the situation into something it's not."

"I'm not." A smile danced across his lips. "How do you think it would play out in front of a jury of my peers? Do you even think the DA's going to indulge the police in their witch hunt?"

"Two people are dead. Tell me what you know."

For a moment, Kincaid's expression softened. "Someone went through a lot of trouble to cover up his crime. I didn't do this, but whoever did wants you to waste time. You need to let me go. You need to look elsewhere."

I went to the door.

"Liv, please." That time, I heard something in Axel's voice I'd never heard before — desperation.

I barely made it to my desk before the phones rang. Not just my phone, but half the phones in the bullpen. The last time something like this happened, we were dealing with an emergency.

"What?" I asked into the receiver, watching Fennel's expression as he listened to the caller on his line.

"DeMarco," it was Mac, "five minutes ago a device detonated inside the hotel. We've evacuated the building and set up a perimeter. But you need to get down here ASAP."

"Casualties?" I asked.

"None. It wasn't that kind of device."

TWENTY

"Jesus." I peered through the gaping hole blown in the wall. "You're sure no one was hurt?"

"Nope. They blew out the back of the mechanical room which shared a wall with the closet in the executive suite. Whoever did this went to a lot of trouble to rob the safe." Mac flipped through feeds on the tablet, showing the mobile version of the hotel cameras. "The hotel security system resets monthly. It's when old data is wiped from the drives. It's automatic. Whoever did this timed it just right." She held out the blank screen. "We got nothing."

I knelt beside the charred metallic edge. Everything was covered in a layer of dust. "Check for cocaine."

"I think that's drywall," Mac said.

I looked at one of the CSU techs. "Yes, ma'am." He reached for a swab.

Fennel joined us, whistling at the damage. "Damn." He rubbed the stubble on his cheek, a gesture I'd grown accustomed to seeing whenever he lost his train of thought. "The bomb squad cleared the building. Fire department checked for structural damage, but it was contained. From the remnants we recovered, it looks like a shaped charge aimed to break into the safe." He flipped through his notepad. "According to housekeeping, the room was vacant. Mr. Hart has a standing reservation but hasn't been back since his car was stolen."

"Again with Hart. His name's popped up one too many times."

"I sent a few unis to pick him up," Brad said.

"Does the hotel have any idea what was inside the safe?" I asked. I'd never seen a full-sized wall safe in a hotel room, but then again, I'd never stayed in a five-star executive suite either. Apparently, these weren't your normal accommodations.

Brad shook his head. "They reset the code whenever a guest checks out. Otherwise, they don't touch it."

"Great."

The tech held up a swab with a bright purple tip. "Good call, Detective."

Massaging my temples, I stepped into the hallway. The security cameras were still deactivated. The entire reset took two hours. The only people who knew about it were hotel staff, but hotel staff should have had access to the room and the safe's override code. They would have had no reason to blow through the wall.

"Whoever's behind this isn't with the hotel," Brad said, reading my mind. He gave my shoulder a squeeze. "You okay?"

"It's not about the cars. It's about what's inside them. That's what Becca told me, and she was right. Hart's an alleged businessman, but he controls half a dozen shell companies."

"You think he's dealing."

"I think he's the supplier. He runs an

import/export company. He's in the perfect position to smuggle in contraband. Becca knew something was up. She wouldn't give me a name, but she knew who was behind this."

"Hart's a member of Kincaid's club. Kincaid could be dealing for him."

"Could be." Becca practically said as much, but I'd never seen drugs inside Spark. Perhaps, Kincaid made it a point to keep them out of sight. "I don't know."

"Really?" Brad's eyebrows went skyward. "Need I remind you he was in the bathroom with the ceiling tiles and the cocaine dust?"

"I know. I just don't know if he's moving them inside Spark. I spent three months waitressing, and I never saw anyone use or deal. It's a club, Brad. Name any other club where you haven't seen pushers passing out X or something worse."

"Maybe you missed it. Maybe they kept it away from you."

"I doubt it, but Kincaid might be moving them elsewhere. It's the Vegas experience. He sets up these events at Spark, and either closes down the club for private events or moves product outside the club's walls so it won't track to him. Fox should know what's going on. After all, he wanted to party with Becca. He admitted as much when he told us about their time together."

Brad thought about it. "Kincaid could be interested in the cars for obvious reasons since he's running underground races, and he can keep his hands clean by delegating the dirtier aspects of the business to his general manager."

"There's just one problem. They're both in custody." My mind flashed back to the bar. "Emilio." I picked up the radio. When we scooped up most of Spark's employees and customers, Emilio managed to slip through the cracks. He could have emptied out the safe while the hotel was evacuating, and no one would have been the wiser. "Who has access to the mechanical room?"

"Anyone with a black keycard," Brad said.

"Like Juan Rodriguez?"

"It looks like we finally know why someone stole the card."

"They took the maid's master key first. Probably went into Hart's room before he arrived to check out the safe, realized the override code wasn't set to the default, and decided to improvise," I suggested.

"No, this was too well-planned. Every step was intentionally executed. Assuming you're right about Hart, someone knew why he was checking into the hotel and what he was bringing with him." Fennel pulled out his phone. "I'll see if the DEA's heard anything."

"Hart and whoever he was meeting must have been using the charity function as a cover for the exchange. Either Hart was double-crossed, or someone else learned about it and decided to rip him off." Squeezing my eyes closed, I leaned against the wall. "They've been in front of us this entire time."

"We'll get 'em."

Unfortunately, that wouldn't bring back Becca or Juan. After several radio calls back and forth, I got Emilio's address. When I arrived, a few unmarked cruisers were parked outside.

"He's not home," a plainclothes officer said, "but we found the white SUV." He pointed to the parking garage across the street.

"Let me know the minute he comes home."

Cautiously, I entered the garage. A few undercover cops were positioned at the exits. We didn't want to tip our hand. The last thing we needed was to scare off our target. A mobile crime scene unit was parked beside a crumpled tarp and the white SUV.

"He did his best to hide it," one of the techs said, pointing at the tarp. The SUV didn't have any plates.

"Did you check for explosives?" I asked. Given what happened at the hotel, I wouldn't have put it past Emilio and his accomplices to have left a booby-trap.

"It's clear."

I grabbed a pair of latex gloves from the box and put them on. Crouching at the rear door, I noted the bloodstains that had soaked into the upholstery. Becca. Swallowing the bile, I moved to the front seat and checked for car keys.

"Keys?" I asked.

The tech shook his head.

"Did you photograph and print the inside?" I asked, spotting the fingerprint powder on the console.

As soon as I got the affirmative, I reached beneath the steering wheel, feeling for the wires. A few sparks later, the engine roared to life. "Come on." I pressed a few keys. "Bingo." The SUV had a built-in navigation system. I scribbled down the previous locations and examined the tiny routes on the map. The car had been stopped near the alleyway where Becca worked at 2:41AM the morning she was dropped off at the hospital. It remained parked for approximately fifteen minutes until it drove across town, detouring to the hospital before going back to the docks. Hours later, the SUV returned to the hospital, stayed for almost an hour, then drove here and hadn't left since.

Scrolling back through the data, I placed it at the hotel during the time of the heist, and after that, it went to the docks. What was at the docks? And where the hell were you before that? I continued to move backward through the trips. But the GPS only stored the last eight destinations. It arrived at the hotel from

Spark, and before that, it had been parked near Juan Rodriguez's apartment.

The killer knew Juan. The murder was intentional. We needed to dig through Juan's history with a fine-tooth comb. Someone in his life had to know something.

"We'll do another canvass, and I'll speak to his parents again," Brad promised after I called to fill him in.

"Show them photos of everyone and anyone."

"You know, my badge says detective too."

"Then why didn't you do that in the first place?" I asked. It wasn't a fair question.

"Bye, Liv." Brad knew better than to deal with me when I was frustrated.

The radio chirped. "We've got movement. Waiting on a positive ID."

I slid out of the front seat and went to the exit. Someone was entering the apartment building. I gestured to the plainclothes officers to secure the exits. They repositioned, and I turned off my radio.

Slowly, I followed the man up the steps. He wore a khaki-colored jacket with the hood pulled up. He had the same build as Emilio, but I couldn't be certain it was him. Khaki jacket stopped outside Emilio's apartment and fumbled with the keys.

"Police," I announced, my gun aimed at him. "Hands in the air."

He took a step back, complying with my demands. "What did I do?"

"Shit." I turned on my radio. "It's not him. Maintain eyes." I tucked the radio away and jerked my gun at the door. "Turn around. Put your hands against the wall." He didn't hesitate to obey, and I holstered my gun and patted him down. "Who are you?"

"Pearson Riggs." He held up the keys. "I just rented

this place for the week."

"Where's Emilio?"

"I don't know. He said he was going away on a trip and wanted to rent out his place. I'm just here visiting my cousins. They live in a studio, so I needed a place to stay."

"How long have you been staying here?" I asked.

"Since yesterday."

"We'll have to verify your story." I nodded at the door. "In the meantime, why don't you invite us in?" I glanced back at the officer, and we followed Pearson inside.

His story checked out. And aside from being frazzled, he graciously let us search the apartment. Since he was the current custodian of the property, the search was legal.

"DeMarco," the officer held up several photographs of the hotel and schematics on the blown safe, "it looks like Emilio's our guy."

"Yeah, but where is he?"

TWENTY-ONE

Fennel and I met up at the station. He'd come straight from speaking to Juan Rodriguez's parents. Brad had shown them photographs of every employee and member, but they didn't recognize anyone from Spark. Like most twenty-somethings, Juan kept his private life a secret from his parents and an open book to his hundreds of friends on social media.

"Mac's scrubbing his data again," Fennel said. "What'd you find at the docks?"

"Water. Boats. A duck."

"And you think I'm a pain in the ass?"

I cracked a smile. "I'm sorry about before."

"Yeah, well, I'm used to you." He nudged my shoulder. "So nothing?"

"Not nothing." I bit my lip and stared through the slats into the captain's office. "Grayson's trying to get a warrant. It turns out Mr. Hart has several cargo containers at the dock which are scheduled to be loaded onto a ship in two days. Right now, we're just sitting on it, hoping Emilio will pop back up. The white SUV's made two trips in the last few days. It can't be a coincidence. Grayson's hoping we'll be able to open an investigation into Hart. The killer targeted him. We need to know why."

"Did we get any info on the white SUV?"

"VIN's been etched off. No paperwork. No plates. No inspection stickers. Nothing. The car's been professionally cleaned. The techs are hoping to pull something off the engine and figure out where it originated, but it's a long shot. Prints on the center console came back as a match to Emilio. However, most of the interior was wiped. Becca's prints were on the outer edge of the rear car door, so she was still conscious when he threw her in the back. From the spatter inside, he probably hit her a final time once he got her in the car."

"I wish she had gotten a hold of the guy," Fennel mused.

"Based on her injuries, she probably couldn't." My gaze went to the stairs, which led to the holding cells. "We don't have much of a case against Fox, but he admitted to soliciting sex. So there's that."

"Have you asked him about Emilio?"

"He doesn't know where he is and hasn't seen him since they left Spark. The exterior cameras show them parting ways, so we can't prove Fox is lying." My eyes traveled to the interrogation room where Axel Kincaid remained. "Axel knows. He has to." I stood up straight and pulled my shoulders back. "Round three."

"Ding. Ding."

Kincaid lazily watched as I entered the interrogation room. He looked like a lion, unsure if he wanted to be bothered chasing down the gazelle. Leaning back in the chair, he crossed his arms over his chest as best he could, despite the cuffs.

"Where's Emilio?" I asked.

Kincaid made a show of looking around the room. "Not here."

"Where?"

"How should I know? I haven't spoken to him in days. You should know that. You have my phone records." The last call Kincaid placed to Emilio was the night I told him his pal had gotten handsy with me at the bar. Axel turned to his attorney. "Mind getting me a latte from the café down the street?"

The attorney snorted and looked at me. "Just remember, you can't question my client without counsel present."

"Liv can do whatever she likes," Kincaid said. "I'll waive my right."

"Mr. Kincaid, respectfully, I strongly recommend you reconsider."

"Noted." Axel jerked his chin at the door. "And don't get me any of that non-fat, non-sugar, soy crap." The door to the interrogation room closed with a slam. "Where were we?"

"I believe you were about to confess," I suggested.

"Nice try, but since you want a confession, here it is." He spoke softly, so I had to lean in to hear his words. "I fired Emilio and told him to stay the fuck away from you. I haven't seen him since."

"You expect me to believe that?"

"I don't care what you believe. It's the truth."

"Fine, let's say I believe you. You've known Emilio for years. Where would he hide?"

Axel assessed me. "He's responsible?" I didn't answer, but Axel was a poker player. Unfortunately, he could read tells. "That son of a bitch."

"Tell me where he is," I repeated. "He double-crossed you. He betrayed you. You help me bring him in, and I'll make sure you get a fair deal."

"I'm not a rat."

I only had one move left, so I laid my cards on the table. "Emilio went through with the hotel heist. He cleared out the safe. He has the drugs. Everything. He's in the wind. You have to cooperate, Axel. If you don't, you're going down for all of it. He left you holding the bag, probably since you pissed him off."

Kincaid thought for a moment, the wheels turning in his head. "I'll cooperate on one condition. You let me go."

"I can't do that."

"Find someone who can."

With a final annoyed huff, I returned to my desk. We weren't going to cut him loose. Not after three months undercover at his club, serving drinks and dancing in that cage. No. He was not going to just waltz out of here, especially when we found the murder weapon in his desk drawer. Sure, he rarely locked his office, but no one in their right mind ever stepped foot in Kincaid's office without his express permission. They were all too afraid of him. Or too afraid of getting caught.

Axel Kincaid was not innocent. He took me to a race. He practically admitted to the illegal poker games in the back room, and for all intents and purposes, he was a car thief. Becca told me a tale of drugs and prostitutes, but without substantiation, the word of a dead hooker wouldn't go far. Axel was involved in some serious shit. I just wasn't sure he was a killer. Something clicked, and I went in search of Fox's phone records.

The text message I had seen about the five cars didn't appear to be about the thefts. In context, it appeared to be a typo. It should have said five card, as in poker. I reread the rest of the messages. They talked about the latest deal, a new deck, five card, the turn, and the river.

"Maybe it's in code." But if it was, I'd have a hell of a time proving it. A new thought formed, and I went down to evidence to pick up Fox's cell phone. I turned it on and scrolled through his call log and contact list. He hadn't heard from Emilio either. I tapped the bagged phone gently against the counter, contemplating what to do.

"DeMarco," Fennel jogged down the steps to meet me, "I just got off the phone with the DEA. They've had Hart under surveillance for a while. A few months ago, they received an anonymous tip. It turns out he gets an inordinate amount of suspicious shipments from Colombia and other parts of South America. They have agents inside the cartels who recall Hart visiting one of the compounds about eight months ago. But they are still building a case, so anything we find, they want access to."

"Who tipped them?"

Fennel shrugged. "How'd it go with Kincaid?"

"It didn't." I let out a lengthy exhale. "He's going to slip through our fingers. I can feel it. He offered to cooperate if we cut him loose."

"What did Grayson say?"

"I haven't told him yet." Because I already knew the answer.

TWENTY-TWO

"You shouldn't have arrested him," ADA Winters said.

"We found our murder weapon in his desk drawer. What the hell were we supposed to do?" Fennel asked. "Throw a party?"

"Yeah, okay." Winters clicked his pen a few times. "I get it, but Axel Kincaid isn't some two-bit hoodlum you can squeeze for a confession. Once he gets arraigned, bail will be set. He's going to walk no matter what you do."

"Right now, he's still our prime suspect," Grayson said.

"Did we get anything out of Marvin Struthers?" Fennel asked.

"He works for a pawn shop that also provides loans on the side. When payment is not made, he collects the items the borrower put up as collateral. Unfortunately, there's nothing illegal about it," Grayson said.

"He was at the races," I pointed out.

"He claims he works those on the side. Gets an

anonymous message with a location and time, and he just shows up. He says he doesn't know who's in charge or who organizes them. He just handles the wagers, issues payouts, takes his cut, and leaves the house's winnings in an envelope at a dead drop. We're keeping eyes on the drop, but nothing links to Kincaid."

"Struthers must be lying," I said.

"We're going to have a tough time proving it," Grayson said.

"What about the tattoo?" I asked. "That places him inside the hotel hours before the heist, around the same time Kincaid was there."

"Struthers isn't the only one with a reaper tattoo. He wasn't at the hotel; he was across town sitting through a driver's safety class. But he did say he saw a few guys at one of the races with basically the same tattoo and decided to get a similar design," Grayson said.

"What guys?" Brad asked.

"Security guards. He didn't get names, but you know the type. Crew cuts and muscles for brains."

"The way Brad used to be," I teased, and Fennel squinted at me.

"Unfortunately, that doesn't get us anywhere either," Grayson said, reeling us back in. "And John Smith's prepaid credit card turned out to be another dead end. Assuming Smith's our killer, he went to a lot of trouble to cover his tracks and conceal his identity. He could be anyone."

"Like Kincaid?" Brad asked.

"Unfortunately, we don't have anything solid on him," Grayson said.

Winters met my eyes. We both knew Kincaid had an alibi for the time in question. We dragged in half of Spark's membership, most of Kincaid's investors, and nearly all of his employees. They said he was at the club at the time of the shooting. It just so happened he had been at the hotel an hour before, just like two hundred other people.

"What about the car races and illegal gambling?" I asked. "Those seem pretty damn solid to me."

"Right now, those are the only charges we stand to bring. And that's a crapshoot. Given the names on Spark's list, Kincaid will get a slap on the wrist. I'd say if you can get him to cooperate at least you have a shot at finding the men involved in the heist and murders," Winters said. "Kicking him is your only play. Plus, it'll give you more time to build a stronger case and get more evidence. Without the cars or eyewitnesses, you don't have anything. And since he has Mr. Almeada and a slew of other topnotch defense attorneys in his corner, they'll spin it to make it look like Kincaid's been actively cooperating and the PD's just holding a grudge for his past infractions."

"Fine." Grayson pointed at me. "See how much you can get out of him. The two of you have a rapport, so convince him to tell us everything he knows."

"He's going to want immunity," I cautioned.

Winters stood. "Let's get this straightened out."

When we entered the interrogation room, Kincaid was sipping his latte. He put the cup down, his eyes sparkling. He believed he won. "Am I free to go?"

"Not yet." I leaned against the wall in the corner of the room, crossed my arms over my chest, and stared at Kincaid. "First, you're going to spill your guts."

Kincaid snorted. "Not so fast." He waited for his attorney and Winters to negotiate the terms before he made a peep. "Emilio likes to blow off steam at Rhinestones. The bouncers are lax when it comes to keeping the guys from getting too handsy with the dancers. And you know Emilio likes to get handsy."

"You think that's where he's been for the last few days?"

"Since he couldn't touch you, he probably still needed to scratch the itch." Kincaid jangled his right wrist, waiting for me to unhook him from the bar. "He's been known to blow a few grand in the champagne room from time to time. And Rhinestones isn't exactly a reputable establishment." He chuckled, finding something amusing. "But you're the police. You should already know that."

"What's your point?" I asked.

"There's a shitty inn which shares a parking lot with Rhinestones that always has vacancies. The last time Emilio and I had words, he stayed there a few days to lick his wounds." He smirked. "Or have someone else lick them for him."

"You wouldn't happen to be telling us this because Rhinestones is one of your rivals, would you?" Winters asked.

Kincaid slipped into his jacket. "Rhinestones caters to a different clientele with a different set of tastes. People who want three-dimensional porn go to Rhinestones."

"So who goes to Spark?" Winters asked.

Axel continued to stare into my eyes, even as he answered. "A more refined crowd," he crossed close to me and added, "with a taste for danger."

"One last thing," I said, forcing Axel to stop in the doorway, "do you have any idea who would want to pin the murder on you?"

"You're asking the wrong question, Detective. You should be asking who do I know who would commit a murder."

Winters finally bit. "Who?"

"You have Spark's membership list?" Kincaid waited for us to nod. "Pick a name." An officer escorted Kincaid and his attorney down the hall.

"Is this guy serious?" Winters asked. "Pick a name. What the fuck is that?"

"He's telling us they are all powerful individuals, capable of anything."

I jotted down a few notes and made sure we were keeping tabs on Kincaid. I didn't trust him. And now that he was free, he might rabbit. With his wealth, I wouldn't be surprised if he booked the first flight out to a non-extradition country and waited to see what happened before returning.

"What are you going to do now?" Winters asked, watching as I grabbed my jacket.

"Follow up with Rhinestones. I'll give you a call if I need a warrant."

"Do you want me to come with you?"

A laugh escaped, and I slapped my palm over my mouth. "Haven't you been to enough strip clubs this week?"

"Strip club?" Fennel asked, amused by our exchange. "Count me in."

I pointed at my partner. "You're coming with me, but we have to stop at an ATM first. The fees to use the machines inside those places are astronomical." I turned to Winters. "I believe you have other things to do, counselor."

"Be careful, Liv."

I nodded and went into Grayson's office to update him on the situation.

Rhinestones was everything the name alluded to and not much more. A small cluster of day drinkers sat around, ogling the women who looked about as thrilled to be here as I was. The doorman tried to charge us the cover, but a quick flash of our badges kept him at bay.

Fennel took off his sunglasses as we entered the

dingy, windowless room. "So this is the kind of place your boyfriend likes to hang out."

I elbowed him. "I'm only saying this one more time. Winters is not my boyfriend."

"Well, it's no wonder when he likes hanging out in places like this."

I glanced back at Brad, who somehow managed to keep a straight face. "You planning on taking that act on the road?"

"We just did. That's how we got here, remember?"

"You need to work on your material."

We crossed the room and made our way to the bar. After showing Emilio's photo to the bartender, he pointed us to one of the dancers.

"Verona Mercury?" Fennel asked as she spun lazily down the pole.

"Who wants to know?" she asked.

Oh, dear god. Why did people always ask that question? I rubbed my face, prepared for Brad to run through his usual bit.

"I did. Just now." He grinned, but she wasn't impressed. For the record, neither was I. "Detectives Fennel and DeMarco. We just have a few questions."

She looked around the room. There was only one guy pressed up against her portion of the stage. "I'm taking a break, Mike. You want a refill, now's your chance." He nodded, left a stack of dollar bills on the table, and headed back to the bar. She held out her hand, and Brad helped her down. "So what's this about?"

"Emilio Rivers," I said. "Have you seen him?"

"Honey, I see Emilio all the time. He's practically paying my way through night school. He's a big spender."

"When did you see him last?"

"Last night, I think." She scrunched her face.

"Maybe it was the night before. My days blend together. I know he's been around a lot more these last couple of weeks. He's been renting out the champagne room in order to show off to his friends. We must have cleared ten thousand this month on him alone."

"What friends?" Fennel asked, already removing his phone. "This guy?" Verona squinted at the screen and shook her head. Fennel flipped to the next picture. "What about him?"

"No, I don't think so."

"How many people were in the group?" I asked.

"Four, counting Emilio."

"All men?"

She nodded. "Ladies come in occasionally, but they're typically in groups or with their boyfriends. And Emilio wasn't exactly relationship material. He's harmless, but he's not quite right, y'know?"

"Tell us about the other men in his group. Do they always come together?" Fennel asked.

She giggled. "Um...no. Some nights it was the four of them. But the last time I saw Emilio, it was just him and his buddy. I don't know what happened to the other two."

"Did he normally drop that much cash here?" I asked.

"No, just these last two, maybe three, weeks. It was weird. It's like he won the lottery or something." She jerked her chin at the bartender who was pointing at the stage. "I gotta get back to work."

"If you see Emilio or any of his friends, give us a call." Brad handed her his card.

"Sure thing, sweetie."

"How much cash do you have on you?" I asked, mentally counting what was in my wallet in addition to the hundred I pulled from the ATM on our way here.

"Sixty," Fennel said. "I can't afford the champagne room, Liv."

"Neither can I. Let's hope the bartender's in the same predicament." I led the way back to the bar. Taking a seat on one of the stools, I smiled at the bartender. "Hey, what's your name?"

"Jimmy." He glanced back at the stage to make sure Verona was back to work.

"Sorry for the interruption. We appreciate your help." I looked at the drink menu written on the glass mirror behind the bottles in neon marker. "I'll take two shots of Jaeger and a top-shelf martini." I slid the cash across the bar. "But since I'm on duty, I'll have to come back for them some other time."

He didn't even bother looking at the cash before tucking it into his pocket. "Anything I can get you now?"

"Emilio's receipts and the receipts of anyone else who might have been with him."

The bartender studied me for a long moment, his gaze shifting to Brad who was leaning one elbow against the bar while watching the girls on the poles, as if oblivious to our exchange. After a few more seconds of careful deliberation, he reached beneath the bar and removed a spike covered in paid receipts. He flipped through, sliding a stack off and handing me probably a hundred receipts. They weren't all from Emilio, but Jimmy couldn't be bothered to filter through them. And for the forty dollars I slipped him, this was a lot more than I ever expected.

"Anything else?" the bartender asked, a slight edge to his voice, indicating he was running out of patience.

"Those drinks sound pretty good," Fennel mused. "I'll have the same, also at a later date." He slipped a fifty to the bartender, but he kept his finger on the cash before the bartender hid it away. "Just remember, I'm a better tipper." Fennel put his phone on the bar and scrolled through some photos. "How did these guys tip?"

As soon as Brad removed his finger from the money, it disappeared from sight. The bartender picked up the phone. "Don't know any of them." The bartender kept scrolling before Brad could take back the phone. "But this loser was a total cheapskate. He told me to keep the change on a $1.98 draft, and he only gave me $2.00."

"You're sure?" Brad asked.

The bartender nodded. "Yeah, but Emilio made up for it every time they were here together, so I can't complain too much."

Brad glanced at the ceiling. "Any chance you have security cameras in here?"

"Nope."

"What about the one at the door?" I asked.

Again the headshake. "It's been busted for the last two years, but we keep it there to threaten guys who get too rowdy or aggressive."

Fennel slipped the bartender his card, and we left the club.

"Who'd he ID?" I asked.

Brad waited until we were inside the car before handing me his phone. I looked down at the image. It was a close-up of our crime scene victim. Juan Rodriguez drank with Emilio on several occasions. Things just got a lot more complicated.

TWENTY-THREE

He couldn't believe they pulled it off. The plan actually worked, even if the police had nearly intervened. Killing Juan was necessary. It wasn't planned. His partners would have forbidden it, but it wasn't about what they wanted. He was in charge. This was his plan. They were lucky to be invited along for the ride.

A therapist once accused him of being a narcissist. Then she called him a sociopath. Those were just labels. He stopped seeing her the next day. He didn't need therapy. He just needed to do something to change his life. It was the situation that was getting to him, not some buried trauma or chemical imbalance. His lack of empathy was due to dealing with privileged, arrogant assholes on a daily basis. They never saw him for who he was, but now they would. Now the entire world would see.

It was a shame he couldn't take credit, but he would keep his ego in check. Leaving the gun in the desk drawer might have been a mistake. He wouldn't make any of those again, just like with Juan.

Juan was the weak link. The parking attendant recognized them. How could he not when he had overheard their plans? The kid handed them all the necessary details on a silver platter without a second thought. If it hadn't been for Juan, they never would have known about the wall safe or which hotel keycards accessed which areas. Juan could have saved himself if he agreed to help them. They could have been a four-man team, instead of three. But the kid laughed it off, believing the heist with a million dollar score was some drunken fantasy.

But it wasn't about the money. He didn't care about that. He had plenty of it. It was about the power. It was about sending a message. And as he stared at the fifteen bricks of cocaine wedged inside the suitcase, the message was clear. *Fuck you, Mr. Hart.* Smiling, he returned to his waiting car. He didn't have to waste his time or energy killing Hart. The cartel would do it for him.

*   *   *

I rested my face in my hands, rubbing my pounding head. "It was an inside job."

"Looks that way." Fennel tossed a baseball toward the ceiling and caught it. "Mac found a few photos on Juan's social media account geotagged at Rhinestones."

"He always paid cash." Slowly, I lifted my head and watched the baseball yo-yo skyward. "I hate to say it, but we never would have connected Juan to Emilio without Axel. You know what bothers me about that?"

"No one's IDed Kincaid or Fox." Brad caught the baseball and rocked forward in his chair. "Still think he's involved? Wouldn't giving up his accomplices throw a wrench into his plan?"

Spinning my chair around, I stared at the empty interrogation room. "To hell with our preconceived notions. Let's start fresh."

"Three men in a stolen white SUV. We can place Emilio inside the SUV, and we can connect him to Juan and Becca."

Flipping through Emilio's file, I reread his rap sheet. He had been arrested once at seventeen for tagging a subway car. That was it. No history of drugs or violence. His parents died when he was seven, and he lived with his grandmother until she died four years ago. The apartment he lived in and was now renting to some stranger he found on a vacation rental site was the only home he'd known for the last twenty years. He didn't have any social media accounts. His phone records didn't include any suspicious activity. Neither did his financials. We pinged his cell phone, but it was turned off. We issued a BOLO for him and his car, a late model two-door coupe, but nothing about Emilio screamed killer.

"Do you think Axel's story about the pros in the motel room is accurate?" Fennel asked. He glanced at his phone which hadn't rung since Mac's update. "Ms. Mercury didn't give me the impression any of the girls really liked Emilio."

"They found him creepy because he is creepy. But like she said, he seemed harmless. Honestly, I'd bet on Fox or Kincaid taking a crowbar to someone's skull before I could picture Emilio doing it."

"He might not be our killer," Fennel said. "He could be the driver or the other thief."

I dropped the file and went back to the stack of receipts. "If he isn't our killer, he knows who is, which means we need to find him before he ends up dead. Break time's over." Handing off half the stack of receipts, I went back to identifying the card owners based on the receipt information and barely legible signatures. "Let me know if any of the names match up with Spark's members or employees."

Brad chuckled. "You heard Kincaid. He doesn't share a customer base with Rhinestones."

"Kincaid's an idiot."

"Is that all you learned after three months?" Captain Grayson asked. He hovered above our desks. He put a hand on my shoulder, hoping to soften the harshness of his words. "I thought you might like to know we tailed Kincaid to the private lot where Marvin Struthers left the repossessed SUV."

"What's he doing there?" Fennel asked.

"We don't know. He went into the trailer office and hasn't come out since." Grayson looked at his watch. "That was about an hour ago."

His words left a sinking feeling in my gut. "I'm gonna check on something. Stay on this. Call me as soon as you get a name."

Fennel nodded, and I grabbed the bike helmet from beneath my desk. Officers had already checked out the private lot, and Captain Grayson determined Marvin Struthers wasn't involved in the murders. But he was involved with Kincaid and Spark. And now Axel was at the same lot. I didn't think he was grabbing a cold one with a friend.

I pulled the bike to a stop beside Axel's burnt orange car, wondering which vehicle was more of a death trap. The surveillance team remained on the street, doing their best to appear inconspicuous in a blue and white cruiser. Kincaid knew we were following him, but he still came here. It had to be important, or he wanted to lead us on a wild goose chase while his friends escaped.

Cautiously, I crossed the lot, walking through the

rows of parked cars and the stacks of various parts. It looked like a junkyard. Property records showed it once belonged to Towers Wrecker Service. But the bank took possession, and a pawn shop bought it when it went up for auction.

The rusty chain-link fence stood menacingly on both sides, deterring vandals and thieves. Well, most thieves. I went up the two steps to the trailer. The sign said closed on the office door.

Knocking, I waited. One hand rested on the butt of my gun, perhaps out of habit or fear. Truthfully, this place gave me the heebie-jeebies. "Police. Open up."

A loud bark resonated from within, and I saw the thick, spiked collar and lead hooked to the side of the trailer. A sign in the window warned of a guard dog. Shit.

A large, black dog, some kind of Pitt mix, pounced against the window. His sharp teeth bared as he continued to bark at me. On second thought, maybe I didn't want to go inside. Through the spittle smeared window, I saw movement.

"Axel, open the damn door. Now." Judging from the hinges, I knew the door opened outward, so I stood behind it. A moment later, the lock flipped. The moment the door opened, the dog burst out, running straight ahead. Immediately, I swiveled around the door and pulled it closed behind me, locking the dog out.

"He better not scratch my car," Axel muttered.

"Is anyone else here?" I asked. I kept my gun at my side and checked the tiny two-room office, but the place was empty. "You know breaking and entering is a crime."

"Thanks for the tip, Detective, but I did nothing of the sort."

"So Cujo let you in?"

Kincaid let out a huff and rested his hips against the drafting table. However, it did little to conceal the mess he made in the office. He'd been searching for something.

"Your tie's stuck in the cabinet drawer," I pointed out.

Kincaid tugged it free. "Did you come all the way here just to arrest me on more bogus charges?"

"No, but I'm reconsidering."

"Call my lawyer. I'm done talking to you."

"And just when I was beginning to think you weren't a murderous thief."

He groaned dramatically. "I'm not."

"What about Emilio?"

His jaw clenched. "Look, Liv, this has nothing to do with me, my club, or my friends. Hypothetically, it's possible I enjoy using my car for its intended purpose. And maybe races aren't the only thing I organize for Spark's members. But whatever is going on here isn't about the games I run."

"You said your members are dangerous men and women. What about your employees? From Fox's rap sheet, I'd say he has anger issues. I wouldn't put it past him to take a crowbar to someone's skull."

"I wouldn't know anything about that."

"Of course, you wouldn't."

Axel stepped away from the filing cabinet and invaded my personal space. He took another step closer, and alone in tight quarters, I took a step back. He moved closer still, but I had backed myself into a wall. He wasn't armed, at least not with a gun. He could have a knife, but with a unit outside, he'd have to be suicidal to try something.

"Do I scare you?" His breath brushed against my neck. "You spent three months working at Spark, getting to know me, my crew, the club members, and you still have so many questions."

"You were on your best behavior. Like you said, you knew I was a cop. And you did an excellent job hiding the illegal casino and betting from me."

He chuckled to himself and stepped away. "Maybe I have a few vices, but that's neither here nor there." He returned to the filing cabinet and rifled through it. "Have you found Emilio?"

"Not yet."

"He wasn't at Rhinestones?"

"Have you ever been there?"

"Once or twice. Not recently. I'm sure you checked."

"Did Emilio tell you that's where he hangs out when he's not at Spark?"

Axel rolled his eyes. "Emilio doesn't exactly hang out with other people. He's like someone's kid brother. Fox and I let him hang around Spark since he's a whiz with maintenance and electronics. He saved me a ton by repairing the HVAC when it went on the fritz. So he earned his keep, but as far as friends outside of work, I don't think he has any."

From what I recalled, Emilio spent every night at the club. Mostly, he hung out around the VIP area. "Is he involved in anything shady or illegal?"

Kincaid found a folder and opened it. He removed several sheets of paper and what looked like several pink slips and tucked them into his jacket. "Like I said, Spark's on the up and up."

"Bullshit." I jerked my chin at his breast pocket. "What the hell is that?"

He smirked. "Frisk me and find out, but it'll be an illegal search. And I will file harassment charges. Depending on how thoroughly you search me, maybe sexual harassment charges, but I'm game if you are."

"Illegal?" I practically choked on the word. "You

broke into this trailer and stole documents. Don't talk to me about illegal."

"I didn't break in, Liv. I own this property." He held up a set of keys. "The company that owns the pawn shop is A.K. Limited. It's my holding company. That makes all of this mine, and you're trespassing."

"What's the dog's name?"

He didn't hesitate. "Spike."

"Sure, it is." I kept my eyes on Axel and called to get verification.

"You don't trust easily."

"Said the thief."

His eyes went cold. "There is honor among thieves."

"Sure, there is." I blew out a breath. "I know the heist and the murders connect to you. And I will find out how. Are you sure you don't want to come clean?"

"This is too much fun. Why would I give up now?"

Fennel came back on the line, verifying Axel owned the trailer. "One more thing, one of the receipts tracked back to Iain Harrington. He's one of Spark's premier members. I already made the request for his phone records, but it turns out we already spoke to Harrington earlier today. He was part of the parade that marched through this morning."

"No one flagged him as suspicious?"

"Nope."

Kincaid's brow furrowed, and fire burned in his eyes. He heard the name, and it meant something to him. "Bring him in," I instructed. Hanging up, I tucked the phone away. My right hand hadn't moved from my weapon since I entered the trailer, and with the look on Axel's face, it provided just the slightest bit of comfort.

"You heard?"

He nodded.

"Who the hell's Iain Harrington?"

"Stay out of my business."

"You made this my business. You and those assholes. So answer the question."

"Just know, if you get involved in this, I can't protect you."

"Protect me?" I scoffed, but he didn't answer my question. Instead, he left the trailer, whistled for Spike, and sent the dog barreling toward me.

I managed to get out of the trailer and lock the dog inside with my limbs still intact, but by the time I was done, Axel had peeled out of the parking lot. His rear tires spitting gravel as he pulled onto the main road.

TWENTY-FOUR

Axel Kincaid lied. Marvin Struthers worked for him. Kincaid owned the pawn shop and the old Towers Wrecker Service equipment. It had to be a front to move or steal high-end items, like exotic sports cars, without drawing unwanted attention from the authorities. It was the best way to move these hot commodities without exporting or chopping them. And since the pawn shop and private lot were listed under a separate corporation which didn't directly link to Kincaid, we probably never would have found it because we didn't know where to look. Axel made a mistake by telling me this was his, and I didn't know Axel to ever make a mistake

"We have forensic accountants going through Kincaid's financials and holdings to see what else he's got on the side. I can't believe we didn't know about this sooner," Fennel said.

"We thought vice gave us everything. We'll know better in the future." I squinted against the setting sun. The surveillance team had taken off after

Kincaid, but they lost him in traffic. Kincaid was furious. He knew what was really going on, and he wanted blood. Harrington's blood. "Ping Harrington's phone," I said. "It's a matter of life or death. Kincaid's going after him. I need to get to him first."

"Hang on." After some shouting, Brad came back on the line and gave me an address. "Liv, I'll send a team to his location. Wait for backup."

"No problem." I straddled the bike and took off for Harrington's last known location. I had no idea how Harrington fit into any of this, but I'd find out soon enough.

Zipping in and out of traffic, I was glad to be on two wheels instead of four. It gave me an advantage Axel didn't have. Dammit. I should have prevented him from leaving, except he sent that hellhound after me. I had no idea what he was going to do, but the look on his face spoke volumes.

More than likely, Harrington double-crossed Kincaid. Fennel would have to figure out how or why. I didn't know who conducted Harrington's interview the other morning, but he didn't say or do anything suspicious. No one from Spark said anything out of the ordinary, and since half of them were city officials, we didn't dig too deeply once they provided alibis for the time of the shooting.

I took a tight turn, my bike practically horizontal, and I gulped. No more fatalities, I promised myself. That's why I had to stop Kincaid, but it wouldn't do anyone any good if I became a smear on the pavement.

Arriving at the address, I parked the bike against the curb and searched for the familiar burnt orange. Kincaid wasn't here. For the briefest moment, I felt relieved. But the nagging voice of self-doubt reared its ugly head. What if this was a misdirect?

It didn't matter. Harrington connected to Rhinestones, which meant he also connected to Juan and Emilio. Unfortunately, now that I was here, I had no idea where to search for Harrington. Backup was on the way, but so was Axel.

"Brad, tell me where to look," I said.

"I gave you the address."

"Yeah, and there are two apartment buildings, half a dozen shops and restaurants, and two converted warehouses. Is this where Harrington lives? Works? What's the deal?"

I could hear the sound of typing. "Harrington lives across town. However, his girlfriend has a place near there. Half a block away." He read the street address. "Apartment 39J."

Setting off toward the apartment building, I asked, "What else?"

"Mac?" he yelled. After some muffled conversation, he said, "He likes to do happy hour at McGinty's."

"What's his girlfriend's name?"

"Kristen."

"I'll take her apartment. Tell dispatch to send backup to the bar."

"Liv, wait."

"I can't. Kincaid isn't here yet. I don't suppose we can ping his phone?"

"Not legally, but just so you know, it's turned off."

I hung up and jogged to the apartment building. Holding my hand over the peephole outside 39J, I knocked. I didn't hear any sounds coming from within, but I didn't want to announce who I was. "Hello? Is anyone home?"

Still nothing.

"A pipe burst in 40J. We need to make sure the water didn't seep into the ceiling." I waited. Dammit.

I banged on a few more doors until someone

answered. "Have you seen Kristen today?" I asked. The woman shook her head. "What about Iain Harrington?"

She gave me the once-over, suddenly suspicious. I pulled my badge from where it hung beneath my jacket.

"Iain hasn't been around in a few days. I think Kristen finally broke it off with that psycho. At least I hope so." She gave the door a suspicious look. "Did he do something to her?"

"What do you mean psycho?"

"Screaming, yelling, throwing things. These walls are paper-thin. They had a knockdown, drag-out last week. It's not the first time that's happened either. He accused her of snooping on his phone. The next day, I see her in the laundry room with a broken nose. She said she got into an accident, but you know what that means." She gave me a sassy look.

"Are there any places nearby Kristen hangs out?"

"That girl's always at the coffee shop across the street. She works there, drinks there, practically lives there."

"Thanks."

I was halfway down the hall when she called after me, "You never told me what this is about."

"Stay inside. Lock your doors. You see Kristen or Iain, call the police and have them patch it through to Detective Fennel."

The burnt orange car caught my attention the moment I exited the apartment building. I unzipped my jacket and rested my hand on my gun. The café or the pub? Darting across the street, I pushed my way through the ever-present crowd at the café, but Axel wasn't inside.

"Kristen?" I hollered over the din.

One of the baristas waved, apparently confusing me

with someone else. "She went to visit her aunt. Took the day off."

Turning on my heel, I left the café and entered the bar. It made the crowd at the coffee shop seem minuscule. A moment later, two uniformed officers entered behind me. With the three of us, it was easier to conduct a sweep. I just finished questioning the bartender, who swore Iain wasn't here, when I caught a glimpse of movement outside the pub. Kincaid.

"Axel," I yelled, bursting through the door, "stop right there." He continued to move at a brisk pace toward one of the two warehouses. He must have been a hundred feet away. "I said stop."

He hastened his pace, jutting beneath the partially opened shutter door. I ran after him, reaching the warehouse just as he dropped the door. I tried the smaller side entrance, but it was locked. Since I didn't have a radio, I used my phone to dial dispatch and get patched through to the uniforms at the bar. Two additional units were on the way, but I wasn't waiting. Given the circumstances, we had cause to enter the warehouse.

I took a step back and kicked the door. Pain shot up my leg and through my hip. Damn reinforced door. The two officers caught my pathetic attempt to enter.

"Get this open," I said.

They grabbed the battering ram out of the squad car and swung. The door popped, and I went in, gun held at my side. The officers followed at the rear, spreading out as we entered.

Only one set of headlights illuminated the interior of the dark warehouse. An engine revved, and I focused on the lights. It was the stolen silver sports car. Kincaid stood in front of the vehicle, a gun aimed at the driver.

"Axel Kincaid, drop your weapon," I barked.

His chest heaved, but he didn't even look in my direction. His focus remained on the man inside the car. In the dark, I couldn't see the driver, but I assumed it must be Harrington. The two men were playing a deadly game of chicken.

"I can't do that, Detective."

The officers came up on either side of the car. One aimed at the driver, the other at Kincaid. "Sir, turn off the engine."

"Talk to me, Axel. What's going on? Obviously, Harrington's done something to you. Let us take him in. We'll get it sorted."

Kincaid's aim didn't waver. "Are you going to shoot me?"

"Don't make me do it."

"Go away, Detective."

My eyes darted from the car to the man in front of it. "You know I can't do that."

The officers tried again to get the driver to turn off the engine, but he wasn't listening. The one on the left approached the car. "Sir, turn off the engine and step out of the vehicle. I won't ask you again."

Sirens sounded from behind the shutter, and without warning, the door raised. The driver floored it, knocking the officer back with the sudden rush forward. Axel fired just as I threw myself against him, knocking him out of the car's path. Kicking Axel's gun away, I raced out the door just as both patrol units entered.

"Arrest him," I shouted, jumping onto my parked bike and gunning the engine.

I wove in and out of lanes, hoping to keep up with the sports car's engine. The driver took a sharp turn, and I darted after him, my back tire skidding and bumping along before gripping the asphalt. I shifted my body weight as I came out of the turn and sped up.

We were in an alleyway that let out on another cross street. The silver car darted across traffic, entering a second alleyway. I continued pursuit.

Who the hell was this guy? He turned left, and I momentarily lost sight of him. I turned again, seeing him approaching an empty patch of road. He turned down another alleyway, and I went after him.

I never expected him to stop short. There was no time to brake. The front of my bike rammed into the corner panel. For a second, I was airborne, launching over the handlebars and crashing down on the hood and sliding. I rolled on the ground a few times until friction stopped my momentum. Dazed, I didn't have time to react before the tire iron slammed down on my helmet, cracking the face shield and sending me into oblivion.

TWENTY-FIVE

When I came to, I was staring up at a metal ceiling. The room was dim, or maybe it was my eyes. I blinked a few times, hoping to clear away the fog, but it didn't help. Slowly, I sat up and removed the helmet from my head. Apparently, helmets save lives. I dropped it to the ground and studied my surroundings.

LED stick lights dotted the walls. One on each side. I turned around to look behind me and saw two more. Where the hell was I? Shifting onto my hands and knees, I managed to stand, despite the sharp pain in my left side.

I reached for my gun, but it was gone. I unzipped my jacket, finding a fresh bloodstain on my shirt. Ignoring it, I reached into the inner pocket for my phone. The screen was shattered. My handcuffs remained clipped at the small of my back, but they were useless.

Peeling my shirt away from my skin, I found my badge. The sharp metal edge was embedded in my side. Wincing, I pulled it out. A whimper escaped, and

I blew out a lengthy breath, followed by a few extra puffs. I was lucky. Aside from the damage the handlebars inflicted, I was mostly unscathed. Now to get out of here.

Based on the dimensions, I had to be inside a freight container. I rammed my shoulder into the doors a few times, but they wouldn't budge. The sound echoed around me and magnified the dizzying headache. I needed something to pry them open.

A tarp and several wooden crates filled the rear of the container. Beneath the tarp, I found the stolen yellow sports car. The VIN had been etched off, and the security system removed. But it hadn't been washed. Dried, brownish-red flecks covered the side. Juan Rodriguez's blood. It made me queasy.

At least I found the cars. I opened the door and slipped inside, searching for anything that could be used to get out of the cargo container. I even checked the tiny trunk, finding half a dozen kilos of cocaine. My thoughts returned to Becca.

Focus, Liv. Shutting the trunk, I tried to break into the wooden crates, but they were nailed shut. Turning around, I placed my hands on the car and kicked backward into one of the crates. My foot broke through the wood. Carefully, I peeled back some of the broken boards. Small plastic bags containing computer parts poured out.

I checked the labels on the other crates. They were all stamped with the name of a tech manufacturer. It had nothing to do with the cars or the drugs. Obviously, someone wanted to use the freight containers to move less legitimate goods. They were set to be delivered to a European port.

Even though I always wanted to go to Europe, I had no intention of traveling like this. Returning to the doors, I tried shouldering them open a few more times. Then I tried screaming. That didn't last too long. The echoing of my own voice made me cringe.

When I got desperate again, I banged against the door a few more times. "Let me out."

Voices sounded from the other side, and for a moment, I quieted. I couldn't make out what they were saying. I pounded more vehemently against the doors.

Someone banged back, startling me. "Shut up in there." It was Emilio.

"Let me go." I took a few steps back and grabbed the bike helmet. Gripping it tightly in my hand, I banged against the metal container again. If he wanted me to shut up, he'd have to make me.

As predicted, he unlocked the door. I pressed my back against the wall, my fingers curled around the lower part of the helmet. The moment he stepped inside, I swung. The hard plastic helmet connected with his temple, and he stumbled. I kicked into the back of his knee, dropping him onto all fours. I struck again, this time to his upper back. When he went flat on the floor, I pounced. Kneeling on his back, I cuffed him.

He wasn't armed, except for a large Maglite. I took the flashlight, knowing it was more powerful than most police batons. My knees pressed into his flesh as I pinned him against the floor. I peered out the crack in the container doors. No one was outside.

"Who's here?" I kept one eye out the door and the other on my captive. I patted him down and removed his cell phone. I couldn't get a signal inside the cargo container. "Answer me."

"Just me and Iain."

"Where's the third guy? I know there's three of you. Where is he?"

"He's not here." Emilio turned his face to the side

G.K. Parks

and tried to get a better look at me.

"Tell me who he is. Where is he?"

Emilio might not be the brightest crayon in the box, but he shut up the moment I asked the question. He tried to buck me off, so I slammed the metal end of the flashlight down beside his face to indicate I meant business.

"The police are on their way. You better hope they get here before Axel does."

"Axel's not coming here."

"Didn't Iain tell you what happened?" From the silence, I knew the answer was no. "It seems your partner is keeping things from you. Tell me what's going on. Right now. We can protect you. I can protect you." He hesitated, so I pushed harder. "You know me, Emilio. I'm the same Liv you drank with and danced with. I don't want to see anything happen to you. Let me help you." I eased off his back, keeping one hand on the flashlight in case he tried something.

Emilio sat up and leaned against the wall of the container. "No one was supposed to get hurt. He wasn't supposed to shoot Juan."

I had so many questions and not much time. "Who?"

Emilio fidgeted, and I glanced outside the container.

"Why steal the cars?" I asked.

"A bigger payday. And a big fuck you to Hart." Emilio snorted and tried to stand. I pushed against his shoulder, shoving him back to the ground.

"How's Kincaid involved?"

"He's not."

"Bullshit. Cars are his thing."

Emilio glared daggers at me. "Axel won the McLaren in a bet. He didn't take ownership yet, but Stevens gave him the pink slip."

- 177 -

That must have been what Axel removed from the trailer office. He didn't want the thefts to link back to him. He must have figured we could connect him to the lot since we had Struthers, so he went to remove the evidence. "Why would Axel steal a car he already owned? Did Stevens refuse to pay up?"

A sick smile grew on Emilio's face. "You have no clue what's going on."

"Stop protecting Axel."

"I'm not." Emilio turned his head and spit. "We're not friends. We're nothing. Iain made me realize the truth. He's my friend, not Axel or Fox or any of those pretentious pricks."

"What about Juan? Was he your friend?"

Emilio didn't answer.

"Your friend's dead. You killed him. His blood is on that car." I pointed at the Ferrari.

Emilio swallowed. "I didn't know they were going to shoot him. Honest. I drove the SUV. I made the devices, but no one was supposed to get hurt."

"Who shot him?"

A sheen of sweat developed on Emilio's upper lip, and for a moment, I thought he might be sick. When he spoke again, he sounded panicked. His breath came in gasps. "Juan knew it was us. We just met him at Rhinestones a few weeks earlier, but he helped us devise the plan. But when it came to carrying it out, he chickened out. Said he thought it was just a joke. A way to blow off steam. He didn't want to help us. He didn't want the money. I don't know what happened." Emilio gasped a few more times, his face turning crimson. He was having a panic attack.

"Breathe. You're all right."

"He'll kill me for talking to you," Emilio squeaked.

I heard a noise beyond the container. "Stay here. And stay quiet." I slipped between the crack in the doors. No one was around. I shut the container and secured the lock. Stacks of shipping containers stood on either side, nearly walling us in.

I ducked into a dark corner between two tall rows of containers stacked five high and checked for a signal. Bingo. Using Emilio's burner, I dialed Fennel.

"Liv, where are you?"

"The docks. Listen to me. Emilio's here. I have him handcuffed inside a locked container. Harrington's here, or he was. We have to find him. They've planned this out. I found the Ferrari and six kilos of coke. It's set to ship to Europe. They must have buyers lined up. I think they ripped off Hart, and if the DEA's right, the cartels too."

"We're already on our way. Get somewhere safe. I'm two minutes out."

Tucking the phone into my pocket, I edged along the containers. I needed to get out of here. I turned the corner and came face to face with the killer.

TWENTY-SIX

He hoped to avoid this moment, but she left him no choice. She should have been dead twice over. But her luck had finally run out. The device Emilio built should have made her car inert. She should have died in the accident. And if Iain had the balls, he would have finished her off instead of bringing her here and dumping her inside the shipping container. But they weren't trained like he was. They didn't understand the risk she posed. He'd take care of it. Like the saying went, if you want something done right, you have to do it yourself, but maybe he'd have a little fun first.

She narrowed her eyes, searching her memory. She didn't recognize him, not at first. He'd spent so long living in anonymity and blending in that no one noticed him. In his line of work, it had been a necessity. But he hated it. It would be different this time. He'd start over. He'd be the one with staff and guards. People would take notice. They would respect him. And they would fear him.

"Recognize me?" he asked.

"You were at Spark."

"Bravo."

She thought for a moment. "You're Hart's bodyguard."

"Head of security," he corrected, unable to help himself.

"Former, I imagine." Her eyes darted to the container. "You planned to rip him off, but why steal the other car?"

"I like fast things." He reached out and grabbed the end of the flashlight before it connected with his skull and yanked it from her hand. She had spunk. He liked it when they fought back. "Plus, I knew you were investigating Axel, so it made for a nice misdirect." He jerked his chin at her. "Get on your knees."

"Fuck you."

He grinned. "If you wish."

*   *   *

I could practically see the headlines now, *Cop Killed with Her Own Gun*. Of course, the story would be even bigger since I was Vince DeMarco's kid. Slowly, I lowered to the ground. My left knee, then my right. Searching my memory for a name, I came up with one. "Mick."

His eyes flicked to my face. His aim wavered ever so slightly.

"I know who you are. I'm just not used to seeing you in anything other than a suit." The ink from an elaborate tattoo caught my eye. I recognized the artist's style. "Kai had the nicest things to say about you. Poor, deluded kid, thought your name was John Smith." If I didn't get out of this mess, I probably just signed Mr. Kahale's death warrant. "Did Axel recommend that shop? I bet he gets a finder's fee."

If looks could kill, I'd already be dead. "What do the police know?" Mick yanked my chin up. "Answer me."

From our brief interaction, I knew Mick wanted notoriety. He wanted to be remembered. He wanted to step out of the shadows, but he also wanted to live long enough to enjoy his new fortune.

"We know everything."

"You're lying." He pressed the muzzle of my Glock against my forehead.

"Are you sure about that? Becca told me about you. About the cars. The cocaine. You got pissed at your boss, but stealing from the cartels won't end well." I needed to buy time. Fennel would be here. I just needed a few more minutes. "You killed her for no reason. We already had you dead to rights. You didn't need to add a second homicide to the list."

"I had a reason."

"It's because you're a pathetic, useless fuck."

He backhanded me. The force of the blow knocked me to the ground, and he straddled me. I grabbed for the gun with both hands, struggling to keep the barrel from pointing at my face. He was six feet and two hundred pounds of solid muscle. It was no wonder Becca hadn't been able to put up more of a fight.

He wrapped his free hand around my throat, squeezing hard. His eyes wild. He was losing control. I kicked him in the nuts. He howled, but his grip only tightened.

I couldn't breathe. He jerked the gun out of my hands, and I scratched at his eyes, shoving his face to the side. Lifting my hips, I crossed my ankles at the front of his neck and forced him backward. His hand fell from my throat, and he punched me.

My vision swam, and my legs dropped. He forced me flat, holding my body down with the weight of his. Somewhere in the distance, I heard the sirens. One more minute. Just one. But they stopped. The sound stopped. I couldn't hear anything over the blood rushing in my ears. He tugged at my jeans and ripped at my shirt. I batted his hands away, and he lifted the gun.

"Fine," he said, as if conceding, "have it your way."

I grabbed for the Glock. The gun went off. The metal burned my palms, but I didn't let go. He squeezed off two more shots. One more frantic than the other. I rolled into him, using my smaller size as an advantage and tucked the gun against my chest. I pinned his forearm with my weight. My back to his front. This wasn't ideal, but I was out of options. He fired again.

"Liv," Brad screamed.

No one moved. Time stood still. I was pinned beneath Mick's bulk as he struggled to manipulate the gun in our hands. Even now, with the police breathing down his neck, he was still determined to finish what he started.

Fennel shoved Mick off of me, and two uniforms wrestled the killer into cuffs and frisked him. Slowly, I rolled onto my back, my ears ringing from the gunshots.

"DeMarco," the bloodstain on my shirt drew his eyes, "are you hit?"

"No, I'm okay."

"Could have fooled me." Fennel helped me sit up and called for a medic to take a look. Several government-issued SUVs pulled to a stop next to the four police vehicles just as Mick was being loaded into the back of a car. "We've got a mess to sort through."

"It's not just our mess," I said.

TWENTY-SEVEN

Brad dropped into his chair and sighed. "What are you still doing here? The captain told you to take the rest of the day."

"You're my ride. Plus, I know how much you hate paperwork." The door to interrogation opened, and I watched Iain Harrington get escorted out. The DEA found him when they were searching the cargo containers. Apparently, Iain heard the commotion and sirens and thought it best to hide. Obviously, he wasn't very good at it.

Fennel had been in and out of the box all day, asking questions and getting everything in order. With all three men in custody, it wasn't hard to play them against one another and get them to crack. Mick Rutherford, aka John Smith and Hart's chief of security, had become disgusted with his job. No one ever tried to make a move against Hart, so Mick was redundant. He was nothing more than a status piece, a trophy wife without the blonde hair and fake tits. Something triggered him, and he decided he wanted out of his life. And he wanted Hart to pay for making him miserable.

Mick met Iain at Spark one night while Hart was enjoying a few drinks, and the two got to talking. On the surface, they were quite different, but they were both unhappy with their lives. Of course, misery loves company. They convinced Emilio he was nothing more than Axel's lapdog, and the three started plotting and planning.

Mick had no reason to wage war against Kincaid, but Iain and Emilio did. Iain had lost bets and races to Axel, and he'd been disgraced in front of their peers. To Axel, it was all a game, but to Iain, it was his life, his dignity, and his livelihood. Iain threatened to ruin Axel even before Kristen broke up with him. She couldn't take the betting and the losing. She called Iain a degenerate gambler and swore she'd never speak to him again. When they broke up, that sealed Iain's resolve to follow through with the plan. Kincaid knew Iain held a grudge but had no idea how far he was willing to take it until the McLaren was stolen.

According to Emilio, Mick was the violent one. He had the gun. He killed Juan and Becca and planted evidence in Axel's office. Iain backed the story, but it was anyone's guess what really happened. All the DA cared about was making a case, and we definitely had plenty of evidence against the three of them.

The conference room door opened, and Axel and his attorney stepped out. "What's going to happen to Kincaid?" I asked. Despite what the evidence showed, Axel was far from clean, but he wasn't our killer.

"You haven't heard?" Brad asked.

"No."

"The mayor called. He's getting kicked. He'll probably get a medal for assisting the police in the investigation. Apparently, he helped us apprehend

Iain Harrington."

"Helped? Axel was going to shoot him. He had a gun. What about that?"

"It's untraceable. Axel says he found it inside the warehouse and picked it up to defend himself. He was trying to make a citizen's arrest when you busted in. But he was too afraid to lower the weapon because he feared Harrington would run him over. That's why he refused to comply with your instructions."

"He's full of shit."

"Yep."

"He can't get away with this."

Brad blew out a breath. "You and I know he's behind a lot of shady things. Vice knows it. Burglary knows it. Kincaid's crossed the line before. It's just a matter of time before he does it again, and when he does, we'll get him."

"Did I hear my name?" Axel sauntered over to my desk. His brow furrowed. "Are you okay, Detective?"

"I think I'm going to be sick."

Kincaid frowned. "I hope you feel better. I just wanted to thank you for saving my life. I wouldn't be here if it weren't for you." His eyes held an amused glint, and he smirked. "I'll be seeing you again soon. Tell the DEA they owe me."

Fennel bristled but did his best not to outwardly react. Something about Kincaid's words and the look in his eyes made my blood run cold. I didn't breathe again until he left the room.

"Let's get out of here," Brad said. "Where are you staying tonight? Your parents' place?"

"God no. My mom would have a conniption."

"The docs said you might have a concussion. You can't stay by yourself, and Emma's working graveyard."

"I'll be fine."

He rolled his eyes. "Come on. You can stay at my place."

We were quiet for most of the drive. We were both tired, and even though we put the killer behind bars, our case, the investigation into Axel Kincaid, remained unresolved. Whatever was going on had to do with Hart and the cartel.

"Do you think Kincaid tipped the DEA?" Brad asked. "It seems out of character."

"He wouldn't tip them if he had a choice. They must have something on him and offered a deal in exchange for his help. We need to question Hart. He connects to everything – the thefts, the murders, the shipping containers."

Fennel tossed me his phone, and I left a message for Captain Grayson. Tomorrow morning, I would confront Hart. But tonight, I just wanted my life back.

"I guess I should start apartment hunting."

"Good call," Brad quipped. He parked the car and led the way upstairs. I hesitated just outside the door, and Brad, as usual, read my mind. "It won't be like the last time you were here."

"Good. I don't think my body can handle dragging you into the bathroom and dumping you in the shower again."

"Trust me. The last thing I want is to wake up under the freezing cold spray. That was just one bad night. It won't happen again."

"You don't know that."

"Yes, Liv, I do. I don't have a problem with alcohol. I had one bad night. It wasn't about the booze. I just needed everything to stop, and that's how I got there." He pushed open the door and stepped inside. "Are you coming in, or are we camping out in the hallway?"

"You know if you ever need anyone to talk to, I'm here. I'm always here. You got that?"

He smiled. "Yep. That's why I had to swoop in and save your ass today."

"Save my ass? Ha." I followed him inside and closed the door.

Despite my protests, he made up his bed for me and took the couch. When I woke the next morning, I felt a million times worse than I did the night before. After a detour to Emma's so I could shower and change, followed by a trip to my parents' so I could get my car out of the garage, we met at the precinct.

A cup of coffee waited on my desk. Just as we were getting underway, the phone rang. I picked it up, surprised to hear ADA Winters' voice.

"I hear congratulations are in order," Winters said. "You put a killer behind bars. Well, two, actually."

"What do you mean two?"

"I just heard back from the investigator I hired. Crane's been identified. He'll be picked up later today. You saved my case."

"I didn't do anything."

"Sure, you did. Let me take you out to celebrate."

"First, you have to win in court, and then we'll talk about it." I hung up, catching the sly look on Brad's face.

"Who was that?" he asked.

"The DA's office." I glared at him. "Don't say it."

"Boyfriend," he muttered, and I threw a balled up piece of paper at him.

"DeMarco, you ready?" Grayson asked, jerking his chin toward the conference room. "He's waiting."

Despite our suspicions, the DEA instructed us to leave Hart alone, but I wasn't great at listening. Luckily, the captain was on the same page. Hart didn't know he was a suspect, and we wanted to keep it that way. He was a victim and potential witness. This was just a courtesy visit. A follow-up to make sure we had our facts straight about what was stolen and why Mick Rutherford might have wanted to ruin his boss.

"Thanks for coming in, Mr. Hart," I said, stepping into the room.

Hart narrowed his eyes. "You work at Spark."

"Undercover." I took a seat across from him. "We just have a few quick questions."

"Whatever I can do to help."

"Do you know of any reason why Rutherford might have targeted you?"

"He was unhappy with his job. Has been for a while. I'm the scapegoat. The easy one to blame for his problems."

"What about Iain Harrington and Emilio Rivers?"

"The names don't sound familiar."

"They also frequented Spark," I volunteered helpfully. "Axel Kincaid seems to be a common denominator. Obviously, the two of you know one another." I waited for him to fill in the silence even though I hadn't asked a question.

Hart sipped some water and looked around the room. So I continued to wait him out. He'd crack. Most of them did. I glanced at the clock on the wall, the second hand audible in the silence. The only thing better would have been a leaky faucet.

"It's Axel. You know him. There's not much to say. His club attracts all kinds. Apparently, even thieves and killers," Hart said.

"And drug dealers," I mused, "or so I hear. Axel has a reputation. He can get whatever you want, whenever you want it. I would think being in the import/export business, that's a quality you'd admire." I flipped open a folder and leaned back. The first few pages related to Mick Rutherford, and the rest were blank. But Hart didn't need to know that. "Did you and Mr. Kincaid ever do business together?"

Hart stared at the folder, believing the answer was in black and white. "We have, on occasion."

I nodded. "Aside from your car, any other property you'd like to report stolen? Keep in mind, we have the men responsible in custody, and they've been chatting up a storm."

"Lies, I'm sure."

"Probably, except CSU is very thorough. And I'm sure the hotel notified you that your room safe was breached. Although, I find it odd that a man with a penthouse apartment in town would bother with a room reservation."

Hart stood. "I think we're done here."

"I'm just confused about one final thing. It'll only take a second."

Hart turned around. "What is it?"

"The fifteen bricks of cocaine we found in the stolen vehicles that were hidden inside your freight containers, did you want to claim those as your property?"

He paled. "They're not mine. According to what I've been told, one of Axel's cars was also stolen from the hotel. Maybe the drugs are his."

"Yeah, maybe. And maybe that's why Kincaid was supposed to meet you inside the hotel a few hours before your car was stolen. But you canceled at the last minute. Something spooked you. Was it the phone call you received from Rutherford telling you you'd been compromised? Is that why you delayed your arrival?"

"We're done. If you have any other questions, contact my attorney."

Hart didn't make it more than a few feet before the DEA agents arrested him in the middle of our bullpen. I nodded at them. We'd bring Axel in for another round, and with everyone involved in custody, we'd finally find out what the hell was going on. It was about time.

TWENTY-EIGHT

"You're running drugs out of Spark," I said. "You're lucky we found you before your bosses did."

Hart glared at me. He might not be a murderer, but he was a supplier who could turn over evidence on the cartels or rot away in prison, wondering when he'd be shanked. The choice was up to him.

Mick Rutherford gave us names and dates, enough to bury Hart, as did Axel. Hart was using Axel and the club to move the cartel's product. In exchange for payment, Hart shipped back exotic cars brimming with cash. It's why Mick thought it best to steal some cars, fill them with product and change the shipping location to a European port instead of South America. He wanted the cartels to kill Hart, believing their import/export man had ripped them off. Then the bodyguard would cash out, buy a nice villa, and become the head honcho. It was a great plan, except the DEA intercepted the shipments, traced the cars back to Spark, and flipped Kincaid.

The DEA knew exactly what Axel was involved

with, and as a parting gift, one of the agents dropped the folder on my desk. Unfortunately, it was meaningless. Axel's indiscretions had been negotiated away. The past forgiven. We couldn't touch him. He was in the clear for cooperating.

"Were we right?" Brad asked, dropping into his chair. It had been another long day. "The underground casino? The stolen cars? The drugs? The girls?"

"Drugs and gambling, yes. Girls, it's not here. And drugs we're blaming solely on Hart, so the only thing Axel's guilty of is illegal gambling. And we're looking the other way." I handed Brad the redacted folder. "Becca would have been able to tell us what was going on inside."

"How'd she know what was in the cars?" Brad asked. "Unless she was one of Kincaid's girls."

"Or she'd been with Hart or Mick and one of them told her."

"Do you think either would be that stupid?"

"Mick killed her. He must have told her his plan. He was proud of it. He wanted people to know."

"Like Juan?"

I shrugged. "Becca must have told him I was a cop since he's the one who tipped Axel. Everything Mick did was intended to thwart our investigation or keep us focused on Kincaid and Spark."

"Like placing the gun inside the desk drawer."

"Yeah, but Mick underestimated us."

"They always do." Brad straightened up his desk and checked the time. "I'm going home to change before I go to your parents' house for dinner. Cover for me if I'm a few minutes late."

"Who's going to cover for me if I'm late?" I asked.

"Emma."

"Shit. I never told her I was going to family dinner.

She's going to kill me."

"Use the bump on your head as an excuse." He brushed against me. "I'll see you in a few."

After finishing the paperwork, I powered down my computer and left the precinct. My car was parked in the back, but a familiar burnt orange sat a few spaces away.

"I told you you had it wrong." Axel leaned against the wall. "My friends and employees are not murderers. I believe you owe me an apology."

"I'm not so sure. If you weren't guilty of something, you never would have cooperated with the DEA to bring down Hart."

"Agree to disagree." He eased away from the wall. "I'm not a bad guy, Liv. But people do bad things. They want what they want, and they'll find some way of getting it. You and I do what we do in order to keep them from acting in reckless and dangerous ways and endangering others. We're the same, you and I. We put on masks and pretend to be something we're not in order to protect people. To protect society at large. It's time you realize that."

I snorted. "There's a line, Axel. And you've crossed it more than once. The next time you do, I will stop you. The DEA and the mayor won't be around to save you again."

"Then come at me, Detective. I look forward to it." He smiled. "And if you or your partner ever want to stop by for a drink, I'll make sure Rick knows to let you in. After all, I'm nothing but a friend to law enforcement. Although, your little undercover operation has left me short a waitress again, so I can't guarantee what the service will be like." He climbed into his car and drove away.

That wouldn't be the last time I tangled with Axel Kincaid, but I had other things to think about now, like enjoying a home-cooked meal with the people I love. I was lucky, despite how difficult the week had been. And I'd never forget it.

Operation Stakeout

A Detective Liv DeMarco Short

Dangerous Stakes

ONE

"Don't I know you?"

Duncan Crane's heart pounded in his chest. "No, I don't think so," he replied.

The man narrowed his eyes. "You sure about that?" He pointed at Duncan, waving his finger up and down. "Crane, right?"

Duncan shook his head vehemently. "Sorry, man. You got me confused with someone else. My name's Lattimer."

The man with the tattoos looked him up and down. "Yeah, all right. You enjoy yourself, Mr. Lattimer." He jerked his chin at the topless girl spinning on the pole. "She's a real looker." He put some cash on the table. "Buy yourself a dance. On me."

"Seriously, man. It's okay."

"No worries." The guy walked away, joining a second man at a nearby table. Something about the two men raised Crane's hackles. He slid his room key and the cash off the table and went down the hallway toward the private rooms. One of the girls just finished giving a dance, and he recognized her as a waitress who propositioned him earlier.

"Changed your mind, honey?" she asked, running her palms over his chest.

"Candi, right?"

"That's right. I'm sweet and tasty." She leaned closer, either as part of her club persona or to encourage him to partake in her side hustle. "Mouthwateringly delicious."

He didn't have time for this. He shoved her into a room marked employees only, just as the two tattooed men made their way down the corridor. He swallowed, watching them barge into one of the private lounges.

"What the hell are you doing?" she hissed, and he pressed a finger to her lips and held out the handful of cash.

"I need to get out of here right now."

"We can go back to your motel," she said.

He shook his head. "Somewhere else. Far away from here. Please." He stared into her eyes, hoping she'd believe him. "Those two men are here to kill me."

*   *   *

The thing they never tell you about surveillance is it is incredibly boring. Most cop shows and private detective novels never allude to how boring waiting can be. I ran through some of the classic noir flicks in my mind, visualizing the smoke-filled rooms, the classy redhead in the tight dress, the detective in his disheveled suit, and the opened bottle of whiskey on his desk. None of those detectives ever got bored waiting around. Maybe sloshed, but never bored. But that was fiction. This was real life, and I'd been on enough stakeouts to know just how mind-numbingly boring they could be, despite my companion's best efforts to keep me entertained.

After stretching in the seat, I took a sip of cold coffee from the thermos and fiddled with the radio. Assistant District Attorney Logan Winters glanced over and smiled. "I like this song," he said.

"You would," I teased.

"What's that supposed to mean?" He shifted to face me. "I'm waiting for your answer, Detective DeMarco."

"I'm not on the stand, counselor."

"C'mon, Liv." He gazed out the windshield.

I snickered, enjoying torturing him. "It's just very you."

"Is that a bad thing?" He cocked his head to the side, his brow furrowed.

"Only when it comes to playing twenty questions." I shook my head and did my best to stop my lips from contorting into a smile. "Who the hell picks aardvark?"

"Well, I won, didn't I?"

"I'm starting to sense a pattern. Life isn't always about winning."

"So what is it about?" He moved closer, reaching across my lap and into the glove box to grab his phone charger.

"More than that. A lot more."

He plugged in his phone. "Agree to disagree."

"Fine." I shook the empty thermos. "We're out of coffee." For a moment, I closed my eyes and resisted the urge to recline my seat. It was two a.m. If I wasn't in the middle of nowhere keeping watch for Winters' witness, I would have been curled up in bed, probably asleep.

"What do you and Fennel talk about when you're

on stakeouts?"

"Work. Life. Our snack preferences." I gave him a curious glance. He'd been asking a lot about my partner, and I didn't know why. But I didn't like it. "Brad brings audiobooks, fresh fruit, and chocolate. And not just any chocolate. The good chocolate."

"I'm sorry. I didn't know the rules."

"Clearly. Maybe that's why you always win." I brushed my hair back and redid my ponytail. "You shouldn't even be here. This is a job for the police, not an ADA."

"Perhaps, but we both know the police weren't willing to make an effort to look for my witness." He watched me from the corner of his eye. "And when I finally convinced them to help, they scared him off."

We'd been over this a dozen times. After Winters lost Duncan Crane the first time, he and I searched Duncan's background, checked his normal stomping grounds, and stalked his online activity and financials. Nothing turned up, and since Crane was a key witness in an upcoming murder trial, it was plausible his disappearance was the result of foul play. That's what I thought, and that's what my fellow officers thought. We didn't have a crime scene, and without that, no one at the station was willing to open an investigation.

But Crane wasn't dead. At least not yet. He was hiding. Running, actually. After a few helpful suggestions from yours truly, Winters hired a team of private eyes to track down Crane. As soon as a positive ID was made, the local authorities were notified. The bench warrant was issued, and Crane was set to be brought in. Unfortunately, things did not go according to plan.

The sheriff spooked him. Crane rabbited, and now Logan and I were camped outside a sleazy motel based on an anonymous tip and some traffic cam footage. It could have been worse. Crane could be dead, and I could be leading the investigation to find his killer.

Normally, my job was to arrest the crooks. It was the DA's job to put them away. And Logan screwed up by not placing Crane in protective custody, but since the new ADA had helped me out of a few jams, I didn't mind returning the favor. Well, at least until the coffee ran out. Now, I was rethinking things.

Beyond the windshield stood the Blue Diamond. There wasn't anything particularly blue or diamond-like about the roadside motel. It took two hours just to get here, and so far, we hadn't spotted Duncan.

According to the motel manager, a man matching the witness's description checked in earlier this afternoon. But we couldn't be sure it was Crane, and the last thing we needed was to spook him again. For a previously cooperating witness, his actions bordered on the extreme. Duncan must be terrified, and there was only one reason why he would be — someone threatened him.

"Maybe he's out drinking." Logan jerked his chin at the converted warehouse across the street. "His ex-girlfriend, Sasha, is an exotic dancer. Obviously, he has a type."

"Don't all men have the same type? Tight ass and fake tits?"

"You'd be surprised."

I raised an interested eyebrow. "You got a fetish or something?"

"Why don't you go out with me and find out?"

"I don't put out on first dates."

Logan smiled. "Wow, I just asked for a date, and you're already planning to sleep with me. Damn. That was easy."

"I'm not easy."

"Neither am I. See, it's just another thing we have in common."

"We have something else in common?"

"We both like locking up killers."

It was a cheesy line, albeit true. I rolled my eyes. My partner had been right all along. The ADA did have an interest in me that went beyond professional courtesy. As if I didn't already have enough problems being the daughter of a decorated, retired police captain. There wasn't a chance in hell I'd date someone from the prosecutor's office. That was asking for trouble, and I'd already had enough trouble to last a lifetime. Regardless, Brad would never let me hear the end of it. Maybe I just wouldn't tell him.

Logan nudged my knee with the back of his hand. "So what did we decide on the strip club? Are we going in? We have two hours until last call."

"First of all, we don't even know if Crane's inside. If he is, he'll have to come out at some point, and we'll spot him then. Second, our intel suggests he's holed up in room 107, so we wait and see how it plays out. More than likely, he's asleep or watching TV. There's no back door, but there is an adjoining room. And without proper backup, if we go in the front, he could give us the slip by going through the other room. Frankly, if he disappears again, I don't think you'll locate him a third time."

"How long do we wait?" Logan looked at his watch.

Usually, the answer was as long as it takes, but we didn't have that kind of time. "Until the morning. Despite being a shitty motel, they offer free coffee and donuts for breakfast. If he's here, he'll come out. He's on a budget and has to eat."

"And if he doesn't?"

"We go in."

Logan chuckled. "Leave it to a cop to clock the

nearest donut location."

I glared at him. "For the record, I don't eat donuts."

"Let's hope Duncan's tastes aren't as refined as yours."

TWO

The night wore on, and I stared bleary-eyed at the motel room. An hour ago, there had been movement in one of the nearby rooms. Apparently, the guests were now checking out after their romp.

I sat up straighter to force the fatigue away. I cracked the window, hoping the cool night air would help, but it didn't. I had no choice. It was coffee time. Logan had taken a bathroom break two hours earlier and refilled our thermos from the coffee machine at the gas station. As I drained the last of the coffee, I glared at the sleeping ADA.

Brad and I always traded off and slept in shifts. It was practical when conducting stakeouts, but I didn't trust Logan to stay awake on his own. He wasn't trained for this. Putting the thermos down, I considered getting out to stretch my legs. It was just after four a.m. No one was around, which would make my presence that much more obvious, so I remained in the car.

Around dawn, a car pulled up, and two men got out. They were dressed in dark clothing. Tattoos covered the small amount of visible skin I could see on their forearms and necks, and they wore leather and chains. I pegged them as being in their early twenties or late teens.

"Look alive," I said to Logan, who opened one eyelid and tried to determine why I disturbed him. "It seems Duncan Crane might have company."

The men crossed the parking lot and started down the path. I sat up straighter, my hand on the gun clipped at my side. They stopped in front of room 107.

"Uh, Liv," Winters said, a slight panic to his voice, "shouldn't we do something?"

"I'm thinking about it."

Silently, I cracked the car door, my eyes never leaving the two men. They tried the key in the slot, but nothing happened. They tried a second time with the same result. One of them peered into the window, but the thick motel drape covered the glass. The man at the door pointed to the number, and they moved down two more rooms.

"False alarm." Winters sighed and readjusted his seat.

However, I wasn't convinced. In the questionable light, I couldn't be certain, but I thought they were packing. I watched the three-room block, from 107 to 109. According to the motel clerk, 108 was vacant, but I wasn't convinced, just like I wasn't convinced the two tough guys weren't here for Crane.

The night turned to day, but the late arrivals remained in their room. Logan was growing antsy. Admittedly, so was I. Something didn't feel quite right. Around ten a.m., I watched the cleaning lady start her rounds.

"He's not coming out." Winters scratched at the beard growth on his chin. "I'm going to talk to the manager again." He glanced at me. "You sure you don't want a donut?"

"No." My eyes remained glued to the rooms. "Grab me a piece of fruit if they have it." The sinking feeling was eating at me. Duncan should have made an appearance by now. He hadn't even poked his head out from behind the curtain, and with the room darkeners, I couldn't tell if he had the lights on or the TV.

My phone rang, and I hit answer. "How was your night with Winters?" Detective Brad Fennel asked.

"It hasn't ended yet."

"Damn, he has more stamina than I imagined."

My jaw clenched. "I haven't slept. You know how bitchy that makes me. So are you sure you want to go down this road?"

He chuckled. "Is there anything I can do?"

"Actually, run a plate for me." I read off the number from the tough guys' car. Maybe they weren't actually tough guys, but they dressed the part.

"Have you spotted Crane?" Brad asked while he waited for the computer to pull up the information.

"No. I'm getting a bad feeling about this."

He let out a low whistle. "The car is registered to Ernest Bering."

"Bering? As in Quentin Bering? The man Crane is testifying against?" I rubbed a hand over my mouth.

"DeMarco," Brad said my name in the hopes of getting my attention, "Ernest doesn't have a record. He's clean."

"Bullshit."

"Despite common sense, we can't pick him up on anything. I suggest you keep your distance. I don't think you should tip your hand, not when you're by yourself." The wheels turned in Brad's head. "I'll drive out and meet you."

"Not yet. I need to make sure Crane's here before we do anything. And I have to find him before

Bering's goons do."

"Cousin, not goon."

"Same difference."

Disconnecting, I watched the maid push the cart in front of room 104. It was the same room the couple used for their quickie. Hopefully, they left a mess. I stepped out of the car, relieved to finally stretch my legs. My body wasn't built to stay in tight, enclosed spaces for long durations, and my back let out a series of cracks and pops.

Winters returned, worry etched on his face. "They didn't have any fruit, but I got you juice or something claiming to be juice." He handed me the paper cup and stood beside me. "I asked about the guys in room 109. The manager said it's registered to an E. Bering."

"I know."

"You know?"

"Brad called. I had him run the plate." I took a sip of the thick, overly sweet liquid. Not juice. Not even close. I handed it back to Logan. "Keep an eye on 109. You see them come out, set off the car alarm. I'll be right back."

Casually, I walked up to the maid's cart, grabbed the universal keycard hanging from a lanyard at the side and a stack of towels, and continued to room 107. Knocking, I called out, "Housekeeping." The *do not disturb* wasn't hanging on the door, which I found odd. I slid the card into the slot. "Housekeeping," I called again as I stepped into the room.

Leaving the door cracked open, I put the towels down on the table near the window and palmed my gun. Neither of the two beds had been slept in. It didn't look like anyone had been here. I checked the closet, finding a backpack with a few days' worth of clothing, and moved toward the bathroom. The door was shut, and I stepped to the side. With my back against the wall, I reached across and turned the knob. It gave easily, and I pushed it open with my foot.

"Housekeeping," I tried again. The last thing I needed was Crane, in a panicked state, to attack me. When no response came, I slipped into the bathroom. A man's razor, shaving cream, and toothbrush littered the vanity. Someone had been here. I just wasn't sure if he planned to come back. I checked the adjoining door, but the inner door was locked.

I left the room, returned the keycard and towels to the maid's cart, and went back to the car. The only way to know for certain if Crane had been in that room was to dust it for prints, but we couldn't exactly do that when Bering had guys keeping tabs on the motel. How the hell did they know Crane was here?

"Well?" Winters asked.

"He's not inside, but he's been here. His backpack and toothbrush are waiting for him. He'll probably be back," I eyed the car again, "unless something happened to him or he got spooked. Maybe he's in the wind. When's the last time someone saw him?"

"I told you the motel manager said the man in 107 matched Duncan's description and checked in yesterday around four p.m."

"All right. Fine." I dialed Brad. Someone needed to get the ball rolling with the local authorities. I was out of my depth and jurisdiction. And with two potential shooters a few hundred feet away, I'd need the help.

THREE

Duncan Crane held his breath and pressed his back against the door. He swallowed, watching the doorknob jiggle beside him. She was going to find him. He couldn't let that happen. He squeezed his eyes closed and kept his body flush with the heavy wood. He didn't breathe again until he heard the faint thud of the door closing. She was gone.

As silently as possible, he flipped the lock on the door, a new fear surfacing. What if she locked the door on the other side? With trembling hands, he turned the knob. It twisted easily, and he sighed. Poking his head out, he glanced around the motel room, but he was alone. It wasn't a trick. Maybe she really was housekeeping. He had no way of knowing, but he couldn't risk anyone else spotting him.

He went to the closet and dug through the hidden inner pocket in his backpack, finding the bus ticket. He stuffed it in his shirt. If he had to run, he couldn't risk leaving that behind. It was his only way out of this mess. His get out of jail free card, not that he would be going to jail. He would be dead. The penalty for reporting a murder. For being in the wrong place at the wrong time. For crossing paths with a gangster. Why didn't he keep his mouth shut?

In less than two weeks, the trial would begin. The prosecutor's case hinged on eyewitness testimony. As a rule of thumb, witnesses were the least reliable but the most compelling. Juries ate up narrative. After all, people enjoy a good story. It's how the human race evolved. It's why movies, television, and books remain popular. And Duncan Crane had one hell of a story to tell. Too bad he'd never get to tell it.

Maybe after the trial, he'd be able to go about his life again like normal. No one should care what he saw after the court handed down a decision. But between the cops and crooks, Crane knew he was screwed. They were closing in, and he was out of time. If it hadn't been for Candi, he never would have been able to get back to his room without someone seeing him.

The dancer made quite the spectacle of herself with that guy she picked up. They'd been loud and sloppy. And the woman watching from the car had been distracted by their display of affection. It's what allowed Crane to crawl in front of the parked cars and slip into his room undetected. Sure, he had to remain on his knees and only crack the door wide enough to get inside, but it was worth it. Or he thought so until someone tried to break-in a few hours later. And now, someone actually did break into his room. He had to get out of here.

The luxury sedan parked out front meant someone had found him. It was just a matter of time before the authorities knocked down the door and forced him to testify. Didn't they understand he wouldn't survive? Quentin Bering put a price on his head. And two men were here to collect.

*   *   *

"What do you have for me?" I asked, sliding into Brad's car. He had driven his personal vehicle and parked beside us in the far corner of the motel parking lot. I wasn't sure if he was being careful or if we were working this off the books. My eyes went back to the empty parking spaces and room 109.

The two tattooed men left the motel an hour ago, but they didn't check out. Since it was the middle of the afternoon, they probably stepped out to grab a bite. The thought of food made my stomach growl.

Brad gave me a sympathetic look. "Did Winters keep you up all night?"

"You mean a single day doesn't have forty-eight hours?"

"Not according to my watch." He handed me a folder off the dashboard and nodded at the district attorney who anxiously tapped his cell phone screen in the car next to us. "That better be work-related. If I find out he's playing *Candy Crush*, I will kick his ass."

I skimmed through the folder. Inside contained details on each of Quentin Bering's known associates. Bering was a wannabe gangster. We thought he was small potatoes until he killed one of his rivals. Although, we might never have solved the murder if it hadn't been for Duncan Crane and his penchant for strip joints. Crane saw Quentin shoot a man in cold blood and toss the gun down the sewer grate. The bulk of the case hinged on Crane's statements and testimony. And due to Crane's helpfulness, Bering wanted the witness dead and would do anything to make it happen.

"How do you think Bering's boys found Crane this fast?" I asked.

"Word on the street is Bering's offering a reward for Crane's head."

"Shit."

Brad grabbed a bag from the back seat and held it out to me. "Thought you could use this."

Rifling through the bag, I pulled out an insulated container with a breakfast skillet. "My hero." I dug through the rest of the bag, finding an assortment of healthy snacks, some puzzle and trivia books, and several bottles of water. I inhaled half the skillet before asking, "What did Captain Grayson say? Are you officially here?"

"In an observation only capacity."

I gave him a weak smile. "It's better than nothing." I finished breakfast and leaned back in the seat. "You sure you want to be here?"

"No, but I go where you go. We stick together. You know that." Brad assessed me for a moment. "You need sleep. You're no good to anyone like this."

"I'll be fine."

He let out a disapproving growl and signaled for Winters to join us. The ADA slipped into the back and leaned his forearms against my seat. "Detective Fennel, thanks for driving out. What's going on? Any leads on Crane?"

"Yeah, we'll get it sorted. Right now, you need to go in there," Fennel pointed to the office, "and rent a room. The nicest one they have, preferably with a view of Crane's alleged room."

"Yeah, sure. No problem." Logan closed the door and darted across the lot.

"You should have checked in last night," Brad admonished. "At least you wouldn't have been stuck in the car all night."

"Obstructed views," I said. "This is the best vantage point, even if we are slightly exposed."

Fennel surveyed the rest of the lot, eyeing the strip joint across the street. "Did you check in there?"

"Not yet. Logan's intel indicated Duncan was here."

"That's changed." Brad reached for the folder and flipped to the last page. "Crane's ATM card was used six times in the last eighteen hours. He must have run out of cash, and since he fled town, he can't borrow more from Sasha." He held out the copy of Duncan's most recent bank statement. There were numerous cash withdrawals from the ATM inside the Pink Lady."

My eyes went to the bar. In the bright afternoon sun, the neon sign didn't look like much of anything. "Dammit, Logan was right."

"For fuck's sake, don't tell him that." Brad grinned. "Since the last withdrawal was around eight o'clock last night, Duncan might have skipped town again. There's another gentlemen's club over an hour away. If Duncan follows his pattern, he might stop there before making his way across the country, one titty bar at a time."

"And if he's still here, someone might have seen him or saw where he went." I reached for the door handle, but Brad grabbed my arm.

"Liv, take a break. Logan just got you a room. Get some sleep. We'll handle this."

Somehow, sending a man into a strip joint in the middle of the afternoon didn't seem like a great plan, but Brad was right. I was used up. "Fine, but the second you know something, call me."

"I will," my partner promised. Logan returned, and Brad took the key and handed it to me. "Winters, you're going to stay here and keep an eye out. If you see the men from last night or Duncan Crane, call Liv, then me. I'm going to follow up on Crane's last known whereabouts." Fennel shoved the folder into Logan's hand. "You might as well read up on the situation while I'm gone."

"Where are you going?" Logan stared at me.

"To take a nap." Assuming Brad's lead didn't pan out, we'd have another long night ahead of us.

FOUR

A few hours later, Duncan Crane peered out the window. The luxury sedan was gone. He scanned the rest of the parking lot but didn't see anything suspicious. He kept his eyes peeled for the two tattooed men or the woman he'd spotted the night before, but they weren't around.

Letting out a sigh of relief, Crane tossed his few meager belongings into his knapsack and slipped out of the room. The bus didn't leave for twelve hours, so he'd have to find somewhere else to hide. Candi said he could stay at her place, and since he'd given her his ATM card and PIN, she owed him. His bank account had a few thousand dollars. It wasn't much, but it was more than she'd make in a month. She could put up with a houseguest for the next twelve hours.

He would have preferred to withdraw all of the cash, rather than give it to a girl he just met, but he couldn't risk it, even if it would make travel and evading the authorities easier. He accessed his account several times the previous night, taking out the max amount each time, but he had to assume that's how they located him.

He snorted. The amorphous they. The police. Bering's crew. Some punk with a crack habit and a load of debt. He wasn't entirely sure exactly who was after him, but with the reward out on his life, it could be anyone and everyone. At least he had fled town and come here where no one knew him or Bering. He could trust the locals. At least he hoped so. He was putting his fate in the hands of a stripper he just met. How fucked up was that?

Pulling the sweatshirt's hood over his head, he left the room and headed toward the bar. He was almost across the parking lot when someone snuck up behind him and shoved a gun in his back. Time was up.

*   *   *

The door creaked, and I grabbed my gun from beneath the pillow and aimed at the intruder. Fennel froze in place, raising both hands in the air. "Easy, Liv. It's only me."

I exhaled and dropped back onto the mattress and rubbed a hand over my eyes. "What time is it?" Based on the pounding in my head, I'd either slept too much or not enough.

"A little after eight." Brad kicked the bedding out of the way and placed a plastic bag on the table. "I brought you dinner."

"What about Crane?"

"He's a big boy. He can buy his own dinner."

I snorted and sat up. Fennel pulled the drape wide enough to see the three-room block across the parking lot. He took a seat, keeping one eye out the window while he unpacked the food.

"I take it the Pink Lady was a bust."

"We know Duncan was there. We just don't know if he'll be back. I spoke to the local PD, warned them about the two thugs Bering sent, so they're keeping tabs on them. And if they happen to spot Duncan at the same time, great. Depending on where that leads, we'll either hang out here and keep an eye out for Duncan, or we'll go back to the strip joint and see if he shows again."

"Where's Logan?"

"Mr. ADA has court in the morning, so I told him to go home." An amused glint played across Brad's face, but he kept the thought to himself. "I'm just curious how you ended up getting roped into this mess?"

"He guilt-tripped me into it. *Think about the victim. Think about Bering's future victims. What this would mean if a killer goes free,*" I imitated Winters' voice and rolled my eyes.

"He shouldn't have put that on you. He's the one who shit the bed."

"He needed help, and no one else would listen."

"You're such a freaking bleeding heart."

"Look in the mirror, partner."

Brad chuckled. "Yeah, I know."

"Regardless, none of us want to see Crane killed, and if he keeps running, inevitably, Bering's men will catch up and end him." I went to the table and picked up a fork. In between bites, I told Brad about the previous night and what I found in Crane's room.

"And you're certain there's no other way he could slip in or out without you noticing?"

"None."

Brad thought for a moment. "We know he was at the Pink Lady around eight. And you didn't start surveilling his room until seven, so it stands to reason he left before you arrived."

"No shit, Sherlock."

Brad pretended to smoke a pipe. "Indubitably, he must have gone to the strip club early, probably for their all-you-can-eat buffet, and went home with someone he met. And since he hasn't checked out of this fine establishment, I'm guessing he'll be back."

"Why?"

"My dear, Watson, he doesn't have anywhere else to go."

A thought formed, and I put down my fork. "Do you think Bering is tracking Crane's financials?"

"It's possible but unlikely. How would he have access?"

I didn't have an answer. Still, Bering's crew showing up last night couldn't be a coincidence. While I contemplated things I didn't want to consider, the same car from last night pulled up, and one of the tattooed men stepped out. He went straight to his room and shut the door.

My stomach dropped. How did they know which room was Crane's? The motel manager swore he didn't divulge that information to anyone. But the men knew to come here and precisely where to look.

"Liv, you okay? Is it the food? I tried to find a decent place, but everything around here's a bit sketchy." He reached across and picked up the container, giving it a sniff.

"It's not the food. Someone tipped them to Crane's room reservation, and as far as I know, no one outside our tiny circle knew which room Crane rented." Thoughts of a leak and betrayal ran rampant through my mind. Maybe the motel manager lied. I didn't want to consider Logan could be dirty or the DA's office had a leak.

"Don't go there. There are other possibilities."

"Like?"

Brad thought for a moment. "Crane could have told

someone where he was staying, or one of the dancers or bartenders at the Pink Lady spotted his room key."

Reaching for the file, I read the intel we had on Quentin Bering again. He killed someone outside a seedy strip joint. According to the facts, Bering wasn't associated with the club, but he might have some type of under the table arrangement with the owner. Maybe he was using the club as a front. And since it was right off the highway, catering specifically to the transient crowd, Bering was less likely to get caught or IDed for his crimes and indiscretions. The Pink Lady was similarly situated a few towns over. But it was the same type of crowd and situation. Maybe Bering had his fingers in both pies.

"Hey, Mac," I said as soon as the PD's resident computer expert answered, "do me a favor and see if there's any connection between the Pink Lady and Rhinestones."

"I'm a little swamped. Give me two hours."

"Thanks."

A few minutes later, a car parked near our room, and Brad nodded to the two men inside. "Looks like the locals are actually pretty good at being inconspicuous. Shall we check out the club?"

"Might as well."

The easiest way to find out what was going on at the Pink Lady was to check it out. Plus, I didn't have any intention of spending another night staring at an empty motel room. Perhaps, one of the girls would be more willing to open up to another woman since Brad didn't get anything helpful out of them concerning Duncan's whereabouts. But he asked as a cop, and generally, strippers knew better than to talk to cops. So maybe I wouldn't be a cop tonight.

FIVE

Twenty minutes later, I stared up at the neon sign for the Pink Lady. It was a large, glittering blue and pink logo with a cartoon drawing of a naked woman, sliding down a fireman's pole. As if it wasn't obvious from the lack of windows that this place was sleazy, they added lights and glitter. After stepping inside, I knew I'd have to shower nonstop for a week just to feel clean again.

The doorman looked me up and down. *Oh, I so want to gouge your eyes out*, I thought, hiding it behind a bright, ditzy smile. The room was dark, smoky, and smelled like sweat, cheap cologne, and coconut oil. There were three stages, each with one or two barely dressed women gyrating and humping the stage or the metal poles. At least I'd been lucky to never work undercover in a place like this. I knew a few detectives in vice who couldn't say the same.

Several men turned to look at me as I scoped out the room. I ignored the looks and whistles as I searched for Duncan. In the dark, converted warehouse, it was hard to make out faces. I passed the bar and heard a familiar voice.

Turning to the VIP section, I saw Logan Winters sitting at a plush, rounded booth, surrounded by three topless women and half a dozen beers. For an ADA who supposedly went home, it looked like he was having a good time. Too good of a time. I wanted to kill him.

I shoved the velvet rope out of my way and stood in front of him with my hands on my hips. Until I knew what was going on, I wasn't going to blow my cover or his. But he better talk fast.

"Oh my god," I screwed up my face, attempting to make it look like I was in an exaggerated rage, "I can't believe you came here. My sister deserves better than a lowlife like you."

"Liv?" Logan glanced nervously at me as the topless women started edging away. "What are you doing here?"

"I don't know. What are you doing here? Shari said ever since the accident you've been having problems getting it up, but really, is this what it's come to?" I sniffed loudly and wiped at nonexistent tears. "I can't believe you'd do this. Is my deadbeat boyfriend with you? I bet you dragged his sorry ass along for the ride, didn't you?"

"That's not what this is."

I turned to the topless women. "He told his wife he was going out to pick up baby formula. That was two weeks ago."

"Pig," one of them muttered, and they all stormed out of the VIP area.

Logan grabbed my hand and pulled me down beside him. "Thanks a lot. I was just about to get somewhere."

"I can tell, but getting locked up for soliciting sex

isn't going to help us find Crane any faster."

He blew out a frustrated breath and tried not to stare at my cleavage. "You're one to talk. Have you looked in the mirror?"

"Fennel told you to go home. Why are you still here?"

"I couldn't leave you holding the bag. This is my mess." He sighed. "Why are you dressed like that?" He eyed the low-cut top and short shorts. "You weren't wearing that before."

"I went shopping." I caught sight of Brad entering the club. "You really should go home. We got this." I reached for one of the full glasses. "And for the record, I'm sorry about this." I threw the drink in his face. "Asshole," I screamed loud enough for half the bar to hear me over the music. The bouncer raised an interested eyebrow but made no attempt to intervene as I strode across the room and ordered a drink.

With said drink in hand, I took a seat at one of the tables near the side stage and put my feet up on the neighboring chair. I could feel Logan's eyes on me. The ADA had no idea what to think, but I caught a glimpse of him stumbling out of the club. The bouncer gave him an enthusiastic clap on the back that nearly sent him sprawling.

After that scene, I had garnered quite a bit of attention from the women, while the majority of the men decided it was best to mind their business since they had a grade A bitch in their midst. I downed my drink, which was a virgin cocktail, and watched Jasmine spin on the pole. Brad was somewhere in the back, speaking to a few of the employees in an official capacity while keeping an eye out for movement. After my little stunt, if Duncan recognized Logan or me, he'd leave in a hurry, and we'd follow him. But no one else entered or left.

"Here." A waitress put a fresh drink down in front of me. "You look like you could use this. It's on the house."

"Thanks, but I shouldn't." I held up some car keys. "I'm driving. I just need a moment to regroup."

"What was that guy's deal?" The waitress leaned against the chair, caressing the back suggestively, probably to keep her bosses off of her for wasting time when there were men willing to pay for more dancing and less talking.

"He's my brother-in-law, who's been cheating on my sister." I looked around the room. "He's been stepping out on her for a while, which is terrible in and of itself, but he and my boyfriend had a threesome. We found pictures on their phones." I sighed heavily and rubbed my eyes. "I thought they might be here together. I just wanted to have it out with that jackass. He still has a key to my place, and I want it back. I know he'll clean me out if he gets the chance. I picked a real winner with that one."

The waitress glanced around. "I didn't notice anyone else in the VIP section, but if he brought a friend, the guy might be in the bathroom or getting a private dance. What's your ex's name?"

"Duncan."

Her brow furrowed. She recognized the name. "The cops are looking for him too."

"That doesn't surprise me."

Her eyes darted to Brad. Thankfully, she didn't realize we were together. "Look, all I can tell you is that he was here last night, but he didn't stay very long." She hesitated, biting her lip.

"He has a thing for dancers. That's how we met, so I wouldn't be surprised if he went home with one."

The waitress looked at me with fresh eyes, as if finally putting two and two together and realizing I was just like the rest of the girls here. I was a friend, a comrade, a sister in this twisted reality. "Candi took him home. She didn't know."

"I'm sure he fed her his usual bullshit." I leaned in close. "I just want my key back. She can have him if she wants him. Although, I should probably warn her." I looked around the room. "Is she working?"

"No." She nodded at someone who was signaling to her from a darkened corner. "I have to go. You know how it is."

"Yes, I do." She took a step away, and I got up and followed her. "Was he here tonight?"

"I don't believe so."

"Any idea where Candi might be?"

"Probably at home."

"Thanks." I slipped a twenty into her waistband and marched to the door.

SIX

When I got outside, I heard sounds of a struggle coming from the side of the building. A woman screamed and begged for someone to leave her alone. Grabbing the gun from inside my purse, I ran toward the sound.

"No, please. I don't do that anymore," she pleaded.

"You're a lying whore. Where is he?" a man with tattoos on his forearm and neck practically spat. Immediately, I recognized him from the motel. It wasn't Ernest Bering. It was the other one. "Your boyfriend ain't coming to rescue you, sweetheart. Either he don't care or he ain't here. Which is it?"

"I don't know," she sobbed.

He slapped her, knocking her to her knees. "The sap was spouting crap about true love last night. Everyone inside heard it. Let me guess. He just wanted to charm his way into your panties. Didn't anyone ever tell him hookers don't have a heart of gold? He'd be lucky to find one who didn't give him the clap." The man backhanded her, and I moved to intervene.

"She asked you nicely to leave her alone. I won't be that polite."

He spun to see me and laughed. "Wait your turn, Bambi. I'll get to you next."

"I don't think so."

He moved closer to the stripper, and I fired a warning shot high and to the right, the gunshot cracking like a clap of thunder. At this rate, I'd be lucky to keep my badge.

"Shit, lady." He raised his hands and stepped away from the woman. "You might hurt someone with that thing." He took a step toward me. "Hand it over, and I promise not to hurt you."

"Well, half of that's true," Fennel said. He held his badge in one hand, his gun in the other. "You probably shouldn't mess with her. She hasn't gotten much sleep on account of you. So she's pissed, and rightfully so." Brad jerked his chin at the ground. "On your knees."

"I thought you said the locals had this handled," I whispered.

"Clearly, I was wrong," Brad said.

The stripper stared wide-eyed at us. I saw the fear in her eyes, and she did the one thing I hoped she wouldn't. She ran.

"You got him?" I asked.

"Go," Brad ordered, and I chased after her.

Her four-inch platforms weren't the best choice of running shoe, and she stumbled and nearly face-planted twenty feet away. I knelt beside her while she examined her skinned knees.

"Candi?" I asked gently.

She looked up, fear in her eyes. "How do you know my name?"

"Lucky guess." I showed her my badge. "I'm Liv

DeMarco. I'm looking for Duncan Crane. I believe you might have been one of the last people to see him." She glanced uncertainly at the tattooed hoodlum as my partner slapped on the cuffs. "Despite what Duncan might have told you, I'm trying to save his life. He can't hide forever. Assholes like that will find him. It's imperative I get to him first."

I offered a hand and helped her up. She teetered on her heels, and I maintained a firm grip on her forearm in case she took another tumble or decided to run again.

Brad nodded at us. "Do you need an ambulance, ma'am?"

She shook her head.

My partner looked at me, one hand on the thug, the other on his phone. "I'm calling for someone to pick him up. Winters is waiting in the parking lot. Why don't you three have a chat in private? I'll find you as soon as I'm done here."

I nodded and dragged her toward the waiting car. Winters pulled his luxury sedan to the side of the building, and we slid into the back. I met his eyes. "I thought you left. You have a real problem following directions, counselor."

"You can read me the riot act later, Liv." He smiled warmly at the girl. "But for now, you should introduce me to your friend."

"Logan, this is Candi." I gave her an encouraging look. "She's going to help us save Duncan's life."

She bit the inside of her cheek and mulled it over. "Yeah, okay. I just don't want any more trouble."

"That guy won't bother you again," I assured her.

"Please," Logan turned up the charm, disarming her with his blue eyes, "we need your help."

She nodded a few times. "Yeah, okay."

In typical Duncan Crane fashion, after arriving in

town, our witness found himself at the not so lovely roadside establishment. The Pink Lady's neon glow beckoned him like a siren. So he went to grab a bite and watch the show. However, Duncan only planned for this to be a brief stop. And since he spent the last of his cash securing a room at the Blue Diamond, he decided the ATM was worth the risk.

"He tipped well," Candi said. "I thought he wanted a private dance, but he told me someone was trying to kill him. I guess that was true." She swallowed, her gaze traveling the path a squad car had just taken. "I snuck him out the back. We drove around for a while and got to talking. He told me he saw something he shouldn't have and was on his way out of state. He has family in Michigan and planned to make his way there."

"When's the last time you saw him?" I asked.

She stared out the window. "Late last night. I helped him sneak back into his motel room. He said people were watching his room, but he had to get in there. He left his bus ticket in his backpack, and he couldn't risk buying another one."

Logan met my eyes. "What bus?"

"He didn't board a bus. He just bought a ticket. As far as I know, he's leaving in the morning. That's why I came here. I thought maybe he'd show up tonight. We could have one last hoorah. He was nice, y'know, which is rare." Her gaze drifted to my badge. "Am I in trouble?"

"No," Logan said.

"Do you have any idea where Duncan might be?" I asked.

Thoughts of the couple from last night played through my head. Surveillance was nearly impossible once you'd been made, and Duncan made us. Dammit. I thought for a moment, trying to figure out how. It must have been the car. Logan's car was too nice for a place like that. But how the hell did Crane sneak out of the room without me noticing? I must be losing my touch. Unless...

She bit her lip. "He has a room at the Blue Diamond. He's probably hanging out there."

"Have you ever seen that asshole before?" I nodded in the direction of the man being shoved into the back of the police cruiser.

"He and his friend were here yesterday. When Duncan spotted them, we slipped out the back. That's when he told me he was on the run." She tugged on the hem of her skirt. "I don't know what kind of trouble he's in, but I don't want any part of it."

"It'll be okay." I hoped that was true. "Once we take Duncan into custody, Butch and Sundance won't have any reason to look for you. They just want to know where he is."

"I'd tell you if I knew." She stared at the motel across the street. "He has to be there, right?"

"I hope so."

SEVEN

"Liv, we gotta move," Brad yelled the moment I slid out of the back of Logan's car. The ADA was going to keep Candi safe until the situation was resolved, but I feared it might already be too late.

"Duncan's still at the motel."

"I know."

My partner didn't wait for an elaboration. He raced across the street with me at his heels. By the time we made it to the parking lot, my gun was in my hand. I clipped my badge to the pocket of my shorts, regretting my choice of attire. Actually, I regretted a lot of things.

Two local squad cars had already pulled up, and four men congregated around the surveillance car. Blood spray covered the inside of the passenger window. The dark red droplets slowly slid down the glass. One of the cops was slumped inside the car. The other had been dragged out and was lying on the pavement while his fellow officers put their first responder training to work.

I froze in place. Then I heard ambulance sirens. Brad tossed a look in my direction. "We'll take the room."

"Careful, the shooter's close," one of the cops warned.

This was a small town. Half the police force was already here, but their hands were full, caring for their dying brothers. I knew they wanted blood, but it was about priorities. We'd handle the shooter while they saved lives.

"Ernest Bering's the shooter," I said.

The cop reached for his radio. "You sure?"

"Positive," Fennel said, his gun aimed in front of him as he crossed the lot and made his way toward the block of rooms. I followed behind, my eyes sweeping the area.

The door to room 107 was ajar, and Brad waited at the side. I tapped him on the shoulder, and he entered. I slipped in behind him, my gun sweeping the area. The room looked just like it had when I checked it the first time.

Fennel moved toward the bathroom while I checked the closet. "Clear."

"Clear," I repeated. I glanced into the bathroom. The few toiletries were gone. I edged closer to the adjoining door. This time, we'd break it down if we had to.

I unlocked the first door, expecting to be met with the locked second door, but it was wide open. It hadn't been like that the last time I checked. Someone was here.

I went in first. The room was set up in nearly a mirror image of the one we just left, only the art on the wall differed. Silently signaling to Fennel, I followed the blood trail. Brad checked the closet. A strangled moan came from the bathroom.

It was locked. We didn't have time to wait. I took a step back and kicked the door in. It swung wide, knocking against the counter, but I moved forward, keeping it from closing again as it banged against my shoulder.

"Drop it," I bellowed.

Ernest Bering jerked forward. One bloody palm coming to rest on the vanity. He considered firing, but his eyes fluttered. He dropped the gun and crumpled to his knees. He'd been shot. One of the officers in the car must have returned fire. Bering fell backward, his hand clutching the side of his abdomen, but I didn't care about him. Brad kicked the gun away, turned Bering over, and cuffed him.

"Get help," I said, knowing Fennel was already halfway out the door.

I crouched beside the tub, tugging on the bloody shower liner wrapped around Duncan Crane. As soon as I pulled it away from his face and throat, he gasped. I released the breath I'd been holding and reached for a towel.

Crane had been tortured, stabbed and cut repeatedly, probably for information. Maybe for fun. My eyes drifted to his captor.

Bering wheezed. "Help me."

I just stared at him. Cops live by a code. You shoot one of us, we shoot you. I understood the mentality. The need. Part revenge. Part sending a message to anyone else with a gun and a death wish. Our lives were on the line each time we went to work. It was imperative we take whatever measures were necessary to ensure our own safety, but it didn't make it right. We had to be better than they were. We were supposed to protect people, not harm them. Not kill them. A few bad apples always spoiled the bunch, and I was no bad apple.

"Help's on the way, just hang on," I instructed. My hands were already full, trying to save his victim. "Did Quentin send you?"

He gurgled, pink bubbles forming in the corner of his mouth.

"Dammit." I couldn't remove my hand from the slash on Duncan's throat because he'd bleed out. "Brad," I screamed. "Help."

My partner returned alone. He knelt beside me, grabbing a towel and pressing it against the wound in Ernest's side. "EMTs are busy. The cops get priority."

"They should."

We did what we could until more paramedics arrived, and then we were pushed out of the way. Two of the officers from outside, who had been first on the scene, accompanied Ernest Bering to the hospital, and I couldn't help but wonder if the shooter would make it there alive. Truthfully, I wasn't entirely sure I cared if he did.

My partner and I stuck with Duncan. If he survived, he'd be transferred back to the city as soon as he was stable and assigned round-the-clock security. This wasn't over yet.

EIGHT

"Are we going to talk about it?" I asked.

Brad glanced at me for just a moment before his gaze returned to the road. We were driving home. Duncan Crane had emergency surgery and had been airlifted back to the city. The hospital was prepped and ready to care for Crane's injuries, and units had already been assigned to guard him. Quentin Bering, who'd been released on bail, had been remanded into custody pending his trial. We weren't taking any more chances, and Quentin's defense attorney would be hard-pressed to find a judge who wouldn't err on the side of caution, given the circumstances.

"There's nothing to talk about."

"There's plenty to talk about."

"Drop it, Liv."

I rubbed my eyes. "I can't. One of the patrol officers is dead. Ernest Bering is dead."

Fennel clenched his jaw, his grip tightening on the wheel. "Eye for an eye."

"It's my fault."

"We did our best. Sometimes, shit just happens on this job. You know that. We all prepare for it, and we do what we have to in the aftermath. Ernest shot that officer's partner, so he got what he deserved. If someone..." He swallowed the lump in his throat. "If someone shot you, I wouldn't think twice about killing him." His eyes snapped to mine for a moment. "And I know you'd do the same for me."

"It's not that." Okay, it was a little of that, but there was something else too. "How did Ernest and his partner know where Crane was hiding?"

"They picked up his trail at the Pink Lady, followed him back to the motel, and waited him out."

"But I was waiting him out. And I missed it. They're dead because of me. That officer died because of me." A tear slid down my cheek, and I wiped at it with the back of my hand.

"It's not on you."

"Then who? Whose fault is it? Logan's? What the hell was he doing at that bar? You told him to go home."

"I also told him to watch Crane's room until I got back. And according to what Ernest's associate said, Crane left the motel at some point after you checked his room but before the shooting. That's why that tatted thug was beating up Candi. He wanted to find Crane and figured she knew where he went. Ernest must have found Duncan in the meantime, dragged him back to the motel, took out the cops, and tortured him in the adjoining room." He sneered at the windshield. "So if you're going to point fingers at yourself and Logan, you might as well point one at me too."

"You didn't do anything."

"Logan missed Crane leaving. That's on me."

I rubbed at another wayward tear. "Maybe Logan

let him escape on purpose."

"He's a lawyer, not a cop. He isn't equipped for recon or surveillance."

"See, it was up to me. And I didn't come prepared. I fucked up." More tears fell, and I fought to keep from sobbing.

"Liv," Brad pulled the car over, "it's not your fault. It's Bering's fault. And he's going to pay for it. He's going to pay for all of it."

Eventually, I calmed. "Yeah. Okay."

Brad rubbed his own eyes and checked the mirrors before pulling back onto the road, the silence heavy around us. Finally, he cleared his throat.

"When I was stationed in Afghanistan, we made routine patrols. I was driving the lead vehicle in the convoy. It was my job to notice trouble." He grimaced as if in pain. "IEDs, insurgents, anything that didn't seem right." He licked his lips, his mouth suddenly dry. "I didn't see it. I don't know if there was anything to see, but I didn't see it. I didn't even know what hit us until it was too late. When I came to, we were surrounded, pinned down by enemy fire. We lost two men that day. I lost two men that day."

I opened my mouth to say something, but one sharp look from Brad forced my mouth closed.

"You're going to say it's not my fault." He took an uneasy inhale. "I'm finally at a place where, most of the time, I believe that. The takeaway here is if you're going to absolve me of that, I'm absolving you of this. It wasn't your fault either, Liv."

"We blame the bad guys."

He nodded tightly. "We blame the bad guys, and we do what we can to break the pattern. No more bodies. No one else gets killed on our watch."

I heard him say that only a few days ago, when we were working the Kincaid case. Now I finally knew why he said it and what it meant.

We drove in silence until we made it back to the city. The ever-present lights easing our internal anguish. It was time for some levity. In a few hours, it'd be a new day. I found a bag of dried fruit in the glove box and helped myself to an apricot.

"I'd appreciate it if you didn't mention that I cried like a little girl."

He snickered. "I'll add it to the list of things I can use as blackmail."

"Thanks, partner." I selected another apricot from the bag. "You always have the best snacks."

"I keep them on hand just for you."

"I'm flattered." I cocked an interested eyebrow. "But why?"

Fennel chuckled. "Did I ever tell you Emma threatened to cut my balls off if I didn't take care of you? According to her, processed food is a slow death, and if I kill you slowly, she'll kill me slowly."

"Sounds like my best friend, but I think you could take her."

"I wouldn't be too sure."

I held out the bag, and he helped himself to a handful. "She's been on a health food kick for as long as I can remember, even before she became a nurse."

"Nothing wrong with that. When I got out of the service, I did that whole primal thing for a while, but you know how work gets." He bit into an apricot. "I'm lucky to find a salad made with fresh ingredients, and let's not even talk about finding a delivery joint with grass-fed beef."

"Yeah, I know. That's why when I work undercover, I just go with the flow. It's easiest."

He turned, finding the tone of my voice odd. "How are you feeling after that bike accident? Still sore?"

I nodded. "It wasn't that bad until I sat in the car all

night with Winters. I'm just stiff and bruised."

"Bet your boyfriend got a little stiff too."

"You should ask the topless waitresses."

"He might have an obsession." Brad ate another apricot. "Are you going to go out with him?"

"Why?"

Fennel shrugged. "No reason. He just asked if I'd put in a good word for him. I take it that means he's pretty serious about wooing you."

"What'd you tell him?"

"I told him if he didn't treat you right, Emma would cut off his balls." His eyes crinkled at the corners. "And I'd shove them down his throat."

"Nice," I said sarcastically. "And my mother wonders why I don't date."

DON'T MISS UNFORESEEN DANGER, THE
NEXT INSTALLMENT IN THE LIV
DEMARCO SERIES.

SIGN-UP TO BE NOTIFIED OF THE LATEST
RELEASE.

http://www.alexisparkerseries.com/newsletter

ABOUT THE AUTHOR

G.K. Parks is the author of over twenty novels, including the Alexis Parker and Julian Mercer series.

G.K. Parks received a Bachelor of Arts in Political Science and History. After spending some time in law school, G.K. changed paths and earned a Master of Arts in Criminology/Criminal Justice. Now all that education is being put to use creating a fictional world based upon years of study and research.

You can find additional information on G.K. Parks and the Alexis Parker series by visiting our website at
www.alexisparkerseries.com